Confessions

Of A Side-Piece Baby

DEXTER SHAW

FIRSTWORLD PUBLISHING
BUFFALO, NY

Confessions Of A Side Piece Baby

ISBN – 13: 978-0-9715515-5-8

10: 0-9715515-5-3

Cover Photos: ©Istockphoto.com

Interior & cover design: FirstWorld Publishing

A portion of the proceeds from this book
will be donated to the prevention and
awareness of Domestic Violence.

CONTENTS

DEDICATION

To my beloved daughter,
Deandra,
and her generation.

QUOTATION

"Infantile love follows the principle:
I love because I am loved.

Mature love follows the principle:
I am loved because I love.

Immature love says:
I love you because I need you.

Mature love says:
I need you because I love you."

~ Erich Fromm

INTRODUCTION

SEEDS OF RAGE

Lashaun Johnson is a young man who is mad at the world and is taking his revenge on it. His mother is the longtime mistress, aka side-piece, of a married man and he is the love child of their illicit union. Lashaun has been labeled a troubled youth; committing crimes through fits of anger.

He holds deep seated anger toward his mother for allowing herself to be a side piece and a burning hatred towards his father for never treating him like a son.

Follow Lashaun as he takes you on a journey through his life from woman to woman, prison to freedom, and poverty to stacks of money. You won't believe a young man could be so cold and heartless or that so many women would try to love him as they do while you listen to the confessions of a side-piece baby.

****

My name is Lashaun Johnson. I describe myself as a poor little Black boy from Buffalo. The truth is I'm more Hispanic than I am Black. I grew up for the most part though in a poor Black neighborhood on Stanislaus Street.

So I identify more with the Black part of me because that's how I grew up. All of my friends and most of my girlfriends as I was growing up were Black.

Living in poverty you learn early that crime is associated with poverty. I also learned early that sexual addictions and sexual predator activities are associated with crime and poverty too.

Crime, poverty and sex have always dogged me, shaped the direction of my life, and are the seeds of my rage. I stole and robbed because I saw rich people with a lot of shit, other people with good shit, and wondered why I didn't have shit.

My first sexual encounter came as an act of molestation at the age of 6 when my 12 year old babysitter, Latoya Richardson, made me her little boy sex toy.

After giving me a bath and before putting on my pajamas she would lay me on the bed and lick on my dick to make it hard. I didn't know what she was doing at first I just knew it felt good.

Then she would take off her panties and hop up and down on me real fast. After a couple of minutes she would kind of scream and fall down on top of me. This made me feel like I was being smothered sometimes.

Most of the time she would get off of me after that, wipe me off with a wash cloth, put on my pajamas and tuck me in bed. Other times she would start kissing me on my mouth before she started hopping her hips up and down again while still kissing me.

She would always ask me "Does it feel good?" I would say "yes" because it did. Then she would make me swear that I wouldn't tell anyone or she could never make me feel good again.

Mama liked to go out to the clubs to party, drink and meet men. That gave Latoya the opportunity to fuck the shit out of me nearly every weekend and sometimes on Thursday nights too for almost two years.

One night a couple months past my 8th birthday she was fuckin me real good. It was like her mind was in another world. That pussy was so good but it was beginning to feel like I had to pee real bad.

I didn't want to tell her to stop because it felt so good but it got to the point where I couldn't hold it anymore. Before I knew it I had busted a nut.

That girl leaped up off me so high she almost hit the ceiling. She yelled at me "What did you do!" I said "I don't know, you made me do it!" Latoya never babysat for me again.

As I started saying before, me and mama were poor. We didn't have much money which led me into crime. There was not a lot of money for food, especially near the end of the month so most of the time, our dinner meals consisted of beans, rice, cornbread and meager stuff like that. Or mama often made a big pot of greens with ham hocks or neck bones.

I liked Sundays because she always tried to make a meal with some kind of meat: pot roast, pepper steak, cubed steaks, pork chops, chicken or something.

Around age 8 mama began sending me to Tops grocery store to buy her meat. One day, as I was deciding which Round Steak to buy based on lowest price, I saw a boy about 16 years old take a steak package and put it down the front of his pants. He saw me see him do it and put his fingers up to his lips as if to tell me to be quiet. He closed his jacket and just walked out the store.

I knew that people stole stuff from the store but this cat was bold and really cool about it. He acted just like everything was normal. After I checked out and left the store I saw a woman giving him money for the steak.

I went up to him and, trying to sound older than my age, I said "Man that was some cool shit. You got paid to do that?" He said "Yeah, I usually just keep the money my mother gives me to buy her meat after I steal it. Then I can have some money to buy what I want. Every now and then I steal the meat to sell it to ladies who can't afford it to get money that way too."

Next he asked "Yo mama sent you to buy meat?" I said "Yeah" and held up the bag a little as if to show him. That muthafucka snatched the bag and ran. He was so much bigger than me that I knew even if I caught him I couldn't beat him up and take it back.

I vowed to myself to get revenge on his ass just as soon as I was old enough. But now I had a problem because I didn't want to tell mama that I got jacked. So, I went back in the store and did exactly what I had seen him do.

From then on, I never bought mama's meat. I stole it and kept the money for myself. I didn't get caught until a year later and had to spend a little time in Erie County Juvenile Detention Center.

I put aside my stealing ways for a while and began earning money the old fashioned way: raking leaves, shoveling snow, cleaning garages and attics, and other shit. I would do anything I could to earn some money. I even had a paper route for a while until I got hit by a car pulling my heavy wagon load of Sunday papers in the street.

Mama sued the driver and got a insurance settlement. I don't know how much it was but she bought me the Huffy 5 speed mountain bike I had always wanted. That thing was pretty and I was proud of it saying (but not actually saying) "look at me" as I wizzed through the neighborhood.

One day I was riding on the sidewalk about to turn a corner. A boy from the LRGP gang, about 15 years old, was hiding behind a bush. He pushed the bike and knocked me to the ground. Then he picked up my bike and tried to ride off. He reminded me of the cat that stole mama's steak.

I had this small Boy Scout type of knife in my pocket. So I jumped up and went to work stabbing this muthafucka in his back as many times as I could.

Here I am; I don't hardly have shit as it is and this nigga gonna try to take my shit! Nah, he had to be taught a lesson for trying to steal my bike.

A man who saw what I did, but not what this punk had done to me, grabbed my knife and held me down until the police came.

I spent another two years in youth detention, this time, in a place called Hopevale. It was like kid's prison out in the boonies where you were confined but you had to go to school, attend counseling, and shit like that.

I got released from Hopevale in time to attend 7th grade junior high school. To try to keep me out of trouble, mama moved us out of the poor neighborhood we lived in and into a more affluent area of the city called University Heights.

We moved to Rounds Avenue just a few blocks from the school that she enrolled me in: PS #80 which went up to the 8th grade.

I struggled a lot trying to get back on track and passed to the 8th grade by the skin of my teeth. On the first day of 8th grade I walked into my homeroom class and there sat Sheila Jemison.

I was stunned for a minute because I had never seen a girl so pretty in all my life. As I was looking at her she said to me "Hi, I'm Sheila, what's your name?" I said "La... (clearing my throat) LaShaun."

We had our class schedules printed out on paper. She asked to see my schedule so she could see if we had other classes together.

Sheila was talking but I couldn't hear a word she said because I was stunned by her beauty and how friendly she was towards me.

Suddenly, everything that had happened in my life seemed to be erased from memory. I felt then like new life must begin in 8th grade. My new life, at least, would begin with Sheila.

Chapter 1

MAD DOG

"Friendship is born at that moment when one person says to another: "What! You too? I thought that no one but myself…"
~ C.S. Lewis

Mad Dog was my best friend. His government name was Larry Winston. Larry was a smart kid who got good grades in school. He was the only child of an upper middle-class family who lived in a huge really expensive home on LeBrun Avenue in University Heights.

I became friends with Larry after I witnessed him being robbed at the corner of Bailey and Highgate by 5 teen aged boys from the Bailey Style Posse when he was 11 years old. They stole his cell phone, $20, and his sneakers.

One of the boys was named Killer Trey. He was called Killer Trey because he drove a kitchen knife into his 6 month old baby sister's chest and killed her when he was only 3.

Killer Trey put a gun in Larry's mouth and pulled trigger. He knew the gun wasn't loaded but he just wanted to have the pleasure of fuckin with Larry on a life and death level.

Larry fell to the ground crying thinking he could have just been killed as the robbers walked away laughing and praising Killer Trey for being crazy.

I was 11 years old also when some boys did the same thing to me. Feeling sorry for Larry, I helped him up and walked him home. I explained to him that some cats like them did the same thing to me last year. Since Larry was barefoot, I took off one of my sneakers and gave it to him so could have at least one shoe.

From then on we became best friends. We hung out and went everywhere together. We were inseparable to the point where you would almost never see one without the other.

We decided that we were going to be predators and never be prey again. So Larry nick named himself Mad Dog but I had trouble thinking up a cool street name. Since I was starting to have some luck with the girls, I simply called myself L.A.; an abbreviation for Loves that Ass. I thought it was cool like LL Cool J! Anyway...

Mad Dog and me begin robbing and stealing doing little boy type crimes at first. We would hit the Mr. Softie ice cream truck because we knew the driver wouldn't get out and chase us. Yet, we took turns being the runner and the receiver just in case.

The runner would go to the window and order 3 cones. After the first two were made the runner passed them to the receiver who would take them and walk away to our hideout. While the driver was making the third cone the runner would take off and run in the opposite direction of the receiver and then double back to the hideout.

We got a lot of free ice cream that summer. Stealing it and getting away after successfully escaping the danger of getting caught made it taste even sweeter.

Another of our favorite crimes initially was taking food, money and candy from other kids after they left the store. We watched this girl who was about 12 walk into the store with a boy who was about 8.

When they came out with a bag of food Mad Dog pounced and said "I got this one." The girl let the little boy carry the bag so Mad Dog went and easily snatched the bag.

Then he saw the girl had a small red purse in her hand that he thought might have money in it. He told her "give up the purse" but she said "No, and give me back that bag!" He said "Give up the purse bitch!" and grabbed her by her neck.

This girl balled up her fist and punched Mad Dog as hard as she could. Before I knew it they were fighting, rolling around on the ground, and that girl was kickin his ass!

Normally girls are concerned about their dress being up and showing their panties. This girl didn't care. She was dead focused on trying to knock Mad Dog the fuck out. The sight of him getting beat up by that girl was so funny I could hardly stand up. But I had to rescue my man cause she was lettin him have it!

I pulled her off of him and threw her to the side. I told him "Grab the bag and let's go!" He scrambled to his feet, picked up the bag and we took off running to our hideout.

There were two submarine sandwiches in the bag that tasted pretty good. I looked over at Mad Dog and the side of his head just above the corner of his left eyebrow was beginning to swell.

Then I remembered the sight of that girl whuppin his natural ass. I'm trying to eat and choke back my laughter at the same time.

Then Mad Dog said "She lucky. I almost killed the bitch." I busted out laughing. I couldn't hold it back no more. I didn't want to make him feel bad so I just said "You a crazy muthafucka man." He was funny too because he always said stupid shit like that.

I could see that we wasn't going to be doing too many strong arm robberies of boys because Mad Dog didn't have the fighter chops. I guess the soft life of being rich or well off kept you living in areas or going to schools where you didn't have to fight.

Knowing how to fight for kids like me was not a luxury but a necessity. You learned how to throw down or else you always got beat down. You stand up for yourself or you get laid out.

Even if you knew that you couldn't beat a fool, if he challenged you, you fought him anyway. If you had to, you did your best to at least make that muthafucka break his hand on your head. At the end of the day you had to make even the toughest cat walk away like half a bitch knowing that he had been in a fight.

Whenever a person has to bring some ass to kick some ass they are less likely to try to beat your ass. They will almost always take the path or pick on the person who will give them the least resistance.

My attitude was, even if you leave me knocked out sleeping on the sidewalk, you are going to have to limp the fuck home. You'll always lose some of your ass trying to kick my ass.

Mad Dog didn't have that type of mental toughness or the physical presence to strike fear in a fool so I figured we had to have a gun to give us the edge. So we armed ourselves and started robbing muthafuckas all over the University Heights and Hamlin Park areas of the city using our bikes as get away vehicles.

We became known in the city as the Baby Boy Bike Bandits. We didn't care who we robbed and were eager to prove that we were not afraid to shoot.

If anybody gave us any kind of trouble, we shot them in either the leg or foot. We started out using a BB gun that looked like a real Glock 9 until we found a

.32 Smith & Wesson revolver that we saw another robber throw away as he was running from the police.

Being a stick-up kid felt good because everybody knew who we were and what we did. But even the adults were too afraid of us to say anything about us to the police.

One day about 5 years after Mad Dog was robbed we saw Killer Trey and another cat coming out of E. Delavan Liquors. Mad Dog had the .32 revolver in his pocket but we had been target shooting earlier so he was out of bullets. He wanted to shoot Killer Trey right there but couldn't do anything except stare at him.

Trey said to the cat with him "Why do young boys try to act like they so hard." Mad Dog pulled out the gun and pointed it at Trey as he was walking over to him and said "I ain't acting muthafucka, I am hard! What's that smell? You smellin' like a big pussy now bitch."

Trey reeled back throwing his hands up and said "If you that hard nigga put down the gun and we can fight the fair ones." Mad Dog said "I have a better idea."

He jumped on his bike and sped away for the hideout to get some bullets. On the way his bike got a flat so he had to ride double with me. We rode down Hagen Street where we last saw Trey walking and found him standing on his mother's porch.

Mad Dog hopped off the back of the bike while it was still moving and fired all 6 shots at Trey putting 4 in the house but 2 in Trey: one in his back and one in his neck.

After being operated on for hours at Erie County Medical Center (ECMC), Trey died before the next morning. Mad Dog bragged for days about how happy he was that he killed Trey but I could tell that his conscience was actually bothering him.

A couple of weeks later Mad Dog and me decided to rob this Arab store on Cordova one afternoon. He would stand outside, keep the bikes, and watch for cops while I went in and took it down.

When I entered the store there was a cat in a white T and I could see the outline of a gun handle under his shirt. I was tired of working with just one gun so I decided that instead of just robbing the store I would take this fool's gun too.

He was acting like he was looking for candy inside the glass counter while waiting for me to leave the store. I thought to myself that he must be planning to rob the store too. I came up behind him, put the gun to his head, and like a cop, I said "keep your hands on the counter muthafucka!" I reached in his waistband and took the gun.

Just then his boy who was dressed in all black lurking in the back of the store came up and drew down on me with a sawed off 12 gage shotgun that he carried hanging on a string under his jacket. I

19

didn't even see his smoky black muthafuckin ass hiding in the shadows back there. I was mad at myself for missing the fact that he was in here.

He barked at me "Put them guns down nigga. Do it now!" Ice water seemed to run through my veins at that minute. Rather than getting excited or scared I got cool. I kept the gun next to his boy's head and cocked the hammer back. I said "No nigga you got five seconds to put your gun down and I started counting down: 5, 4, 3, 2... On 2 I pulled the trigger and his boy's head exploded.

I knew the shock of suddenly hearing the gun go off and seeing his boy's head explode would give me a 3 second edge. So as soon as I pulled the trigger killing his boy I began moving to my right while firing several shots from his boy's gun into his chest. He went down hard.

His shotgun went off but I had already moved out of the line of fire. I was relieved that he had slugs and not buck shot the gun. Buck shot sprays so even if you get out of the way you could still get hit with some of the spray.

I snatched the shotgun and then made the store clerk give me the money. When I turned to dash out the door Mad Dog was standing in the doorway frozen and shaking looking like he was in shock. I yelled at him "Let's go nigga!" He came to himself quick after I pressed the side of the .32 against his stomach for him to hide it in his waistband.

Before leaving I turned to the clerk and said "Say anything to the police about us and how we rollin and I will come back, kill you, murder your family, and burn this muthafucka down! You hear me?" "Yes, yes, yes" he said.

We hopped on the bikes and dashed through McCarthy Park, over to E. Amherst, down Clarence to Kensington and up Olympic to our hideout off East Delavan.

The take was $427 which wasn't a lot but not too bad. I gave Mad Dog $200 and kept $227. He knew I could have died in that store so he didn't have a problem with that.

The good thing was we now had two more guns. The bad thing was those boys were members of the Gangster Disciples. Their boys pressed the store owner to give up our description. They heard about our rep in the area and figured, although they were not sure, that it might be us.

The one thing everybody also knew about us is we didn't fuck with drug boys. I had a feeling these boys might be affiliated and anticipated that we might need a street alibi.

So we left the hideout quickly and took down the Vietnamese nail shop on E. Delavan. We beat the owner bloody so it would make the news. This way when the street started talking about us being on Cordova everybody else would know that we were over here.

21

We got almost $1,000 that day between the store and nail shop and decided to lay low. About 3 weeks later, after running out of money, we decided to do a robbery to get money to take a joy ride. But we got pinched on that robbery and was sentenced to prison: me for two years and Mad Dog for twelve.

Mad Dog wound up doing only 8 of his twelve. Within a couple months of being out he was doing robberies again. His dad had died while he was locked up and he was living with his mom. She noticed that he had money but no job and told him she knew he was doing robberies again. She warned him "That is going to be the death of you son!"

Mad Dog didn't care because he liked the feel of the power. You see, since he was not a fighter he had gotten bitched out in prison. So he was mad at the world and wanted to get some sense of power over his life back.

His end came when he went back to rob the Vietnamese store at Northland and Scheule. Just like I had taught him he was still using revolvers to commit his robberies. He walked in and waived the gun at the owner's son who was behind the counter and yelled "Gimme the money!"

For some reason he fired a shot at the boy but in doing so caused himself to be distracted from the fact that the boy's father was sneaking up behind him with a gun. Just as the son handed him the money, POW, the father shot him in the back of his head. He died in a pool of his own blood with a gun in his hand and money spread out over his body.

As I paused to think about my boy's life, I said "That was not a bad way for him to go out. Quick and painless; doing what he liked to do and feeling powerful the way he liked to feel."

****

Like most good kids with a soft heart who suddenly turn to crime Larry Winston really wasn't cut out to be a criminal. He was simply a victim of circumstances where the trauma of being jumped or robbed damages a young boy psychologically.

It is a type of Post Traumatic Stress Disorder (PTSD) that some call: the Oldest or the Only Syndrome.

This syndrome is where a young boy who is either the oldest or the only boy (sometimes the middle son) in a family is jumped or robbed on the street and it causes the Golden Rule to be reversed in his head. He now seeks to do unto others what was done unto him.

So he teams up with other boys who are into crime to protect himself and/or his younger siblings and begins to victimize other people as he was victimized.

His family knows that he is really a good kid at heart so they can't figure out why he is suddenly drawn to crime. The reason the family has a hard time figuring it out is because the boy is usually too embarrassed or too traumatized to tell them what happened to him.

Larry Winston wasn't really Mad Dog at all. He was simply a good kid that suffered from PTSD. He wasn't really a robber in his heart but he was doing robberies because he was suffering from a traumatic psychological injury.

****

Mad Dog was my muthafuckin dog though! But the muthafucka is gone and now I am on my own. Rest in peace nigga, rest in peace... Oh well, can't stop to think about death anymore. I still got to deal with this life. Living is expensive so I got to keep pushing to get paper to support my living.

Chapter 2

SHEILA

*"The world and all things in it are valuable
but the most valuable thing in the world
is a virtuous woman."*
~ Muhammad

Sheila Jemison is the only child of Frank and Jelissa Jemison who are the Pastor and First Lady of New Life Christian Church. Sheila was a good girl, as PK's are expected to be. She was highly intelligent, very pretty, well spoken, and fashionable.

Her hair was long (just below her shoulders) and jet black with no tracks which complemented her clear high yellow skin tone. Sheila always wore her hair straight or what she called "pressed for success" with either a part down the middle or on one side.

She has lovely personality and is nice to everybody. All the girls in school love her. Even the ratchet chicks that would normally hate a girl like her loved her. She made everyone feel special. Her motto, which she learned from her daddy, was "You don't have to be friends with everybody but you have a duty to be friendly with every person you see."

Sheila was the most popular girl at McKinley High School who was dating, and had been since 8th grade, one of the most popular boys in school: Lashaun Johnson.

Lashaun was a very good athlete. As a Freshman he tried out for the Junior Varsity football team, played one game, and was sent up to play with the Varsity team. He was fast, had good hands catching the ball, and tackled hard on top of it.

The coach couldn't decide if he wanted him to play wide receiver or defensive back. After trying him in both positions and seeing that he was really good, he had him play both.

When Lashaun tried out for the Track Team the coach had the same problem. Lashaun was good at many track and field events except for the pole vault, shock put or the 100 and 200 meter dash.

For some reason he had a mental block against reacting to the starter gun quickly and was always slow getting out of the starting blocks. That aside, the coach used him in the high and intermediate hurtle events, 400 and 800 meter runs and relays, the high jump, long & triple jump, and sometimes the mile run.

In a track meet the more number one and two place winners a team had the more points they received and, of course, the more likely they were to win the meet. Each person could run 3 events per meet. So the coach would schedule Lashaun for any 2 events where he knew he could get a first or second place in during that meet.

However, Lashaun always ran the intermediate hurtles because that was his best event. He was almost the fastest boy in the city in that one and always came in first.

His basketball tryouts led that coach to try a new experiment. Lashaun was 6'1" and 175 pounds as a freshman. That is about as tall as you get, with a few exceptions, as a high school freshman player. Therefore, most of the boys his height played either Center or Forward.

The average high school guard stood between 5'2" and 5'7". Lashaun was fast, a good shooter, and a great passer. He played like a guard in the body of a Center or Forward. No one that tall had ever played guard before at McKinley but the coach decided to play him at position.

Lashaun was blasting baskets and passes over the heads of the smaller guards like they weren't even there. He helped lead them to championships in his freshman and sophomore years.

As you would expect, being handsome and athletic, Lashaun got a lot of attention (and sex) from several girls. Sheila found out, of course, but she was crazy about him and didn't want to give him up.

She had the ideal of saving herself for marriage and family but felt pressure to have sex in order to keep her sex crazed boyfriend. As a result, she became pregnant at 16.

****

Sheila walked into the kitchen one Saturday where her mom was sitting reading the morning paper with a positive pregnancy test strip in her hand. She said "Mom, I have something to tell you." Her mother, hearing the trembling in Sheila's voice, quickly put down the paper and said "What is it child?"

When she saw what Sheila had in her hand she stood up and said "No, baby!" hugged her and began crying. They both stood there crying and embracing for a few minutes.

Then her mom said "We have to get you an appointment real fast so a doctor can tell us what's really going on. Sometimes these strips can be wrong. In the meantime, we won't say anything to your father until we know for sure." "Thanks, I love you mom" Sheila said. "I love you too baby."

Sheila and her mom visited the doctor the following Tuesday who confirmed that she was nearly 8 weeks pregnant. When her father came home she and her mother were waiting for him in the living room and Sheila was crying.

"What's wrong baby" he said to his wife as he was walking over to Sheila. Jelissa said firmly "Frank, look at me." "What?" he said.

"Come over here and sit down" she said grabbing his hand and leading him over to the couch. "What is going on?" he asked looking over at Sheila. Turning his head toward her face Jelissa said "Our baby is going to have a baby."

"What!" Frank said while trying to jump to his feet but Jelissa grabbed his arm and pulled him back down.

"Frank, we have to discuss this calmly, she said. "Calmly, my ass" Frank barked. "Who is the boy!" He looked at Sheila "Who is the boy damn it?"

"Lashaun Johnson" she answered. He said "LaShaun Johnson, Lashaun Johnson, La…, what, that muthafuckin' football player?" He threw up his hands and said "You gotta be kidding me! My little girl gets knocked up by the star high school football player. What the fuck!"

Jelissa said "Frank, please calm down. She feels bad enough already. She needs her daddy!" "Yeah, you're right honey. She needs her daddy. She needs her daddy to beat the shit out of this little bastard who is probably humppin some other daddy's little girl right now.

I am not going to let this lil nigga get away without standing up to me and taking responsibility for this shit. Call that muthafucka up and get him over here!" "Frank stop!" Jelissa said. "No, Sheila, call that boy and get his ass over here right now!"

****

When Frank saw me coming up the walkway he grabed a metal baseball bat and dashed out the door. Jelissa went after him screaming "No Frank!" Sheila was on her mom's heels also screaming "No daddy!" They both grabbed one of his arms each with a death grip and refused to let go causing all three of them to fall to the ground.

After the fall, Frank noticed some of the neighbors were watching. This seemed to calm him down. He looked up at me and said "Get in the house boy, we have to talk."

Frank hit his knee on the sidewalk so he was limping as he went back up the walkway. Sheila asked "Are you ok daddy?" He put his arm around her shoulder and said "I'm ok baby."

When Frank entered the door I was standing in the middle of the living room because I wasn't sure of what to do. "Sit down" he told me. I stated to move toward his recliner. "Not there, muthafucka, over there" he said pointing to the chair Sheila had been sitting in. Sheila and her mother were huddled together on the couch.

Frank sat next to Jelissa and said to me "So, what do you have to say for yourself?" "I'm stupid?" I replied. "16 year old boys have a habit of doing stupid stuff. I didn't realize just how stupid I was being until Sheila told me she is having a baby." "SHE is having a baby?" Frank said. "I mean we, we are having a baby."

"So what do you plan to do? How do you plan to support this child?" Frank asked. "I don't know. I haven't had a chance think about it yet. I know I have to support it. I just don't know what I'm going to do right now" I answered.

Frank said "Here's what you are going to do. You are going to stay the fuck away from my daughter. I will take care of this baby because you have no clue about how to be a father so you will just fuck it up.

It is clear to me that you can't take responsibility for a baby because you haven't got response ability. So I am not going to allow you to be responsible for a child when it is obvious that you are not response able!

If I ever see or hear of you being anywhere near Sheila ever again, I will not be responsible for what I do to you. Do you understand me?" Frank said. "I said "Yes, but…"

Frank cut me off and asked again "Do you understand me lil' nigga?" "Yes, sir" I said. "Now, get the fuck out of my house!" he said staring at me as if he was planning in his mind on how to kill me.

In spite of the warning, I was still seeing Sheila but it was not all my fault. She still wanted to see me and frequently asked me to sneak over to her house at night.

As I was getting ready to leave one night a neighbor called and told Frank that a boy was at their back window and may be trying to break in.

Frank caught me trying to sneak down the driveway and stopped me at gun point. He said "Get your ass back up the driveway. You must have thought I was playing with yo monkey ass." "But Mr. Jemison..." "But my ass lil nigga shut up and walk."

****

Frank had an old 1965 Chevy Nova that he'd been working on that had bench seats and no seat belts. He forced Lashaun into the car from the driver side and took him for a ride.

Frank drove him out to a dark stretch of country highway. Then he explained the real reason he wanted Lashaun to stay away from Sheila.

****

"I know who you really are" Frank said. "I know you because I used to be you. I used to go around fuckin every little girl and woman in town and I got a few pregnant too. Fortunately for me but unfortunately for them, most of them got abortions.

However, when I met my wife, who is the best woman I ever had in my life, and got her pregnant I knew that I had to change.

I always had spirituality about me. I loved to read and study the Bible but I also loved pussy quite a bit more than I loved the Lord.

You see, I grew up without a father too so I didn't have a man around to teach me how to regulate my shit. But once Jelissa told me that she was pregnant, it was like my head opened up and now I could hear GOD speaking directly to me.

HE said "Your next child is going to a daughter. If you don't change your ways, all the sins you committed with women will be passed on to her." I knew Jelissa wasn't the type to have an abortion plus I loved her and wanted to marry her. So to protect my daughter I immediately changed and stopped my dogish ways. When my baby girl was born I knew right then that I had to dedicate my life to a service to the Lord.

I realize that in some ways Sheila getting pregnant is my fault. The seeds of sin in the father are passed on to the children. Perhaps if I had been cleansed of my sinful ways before she had been conceived of my seed things would be different and she would have never met you.

But the one fact about GOD that most Christians are unaware of is HE makes us pay for our sins while we are living not in hell after we are dead. Therefore, my baby girl's sin is sown of my seed and is therefore on me.

So, I am going to take responsibility for what she did and hope that she turns the sin nature that she inherited from me into a success story. However, I know that she cannot do that if you are still around.

Like I said, I used to be you so I know you muthafucka. You still have the seed of corruption in your heart and in your loins. Every time you touch her you pass on some of what is in you into her. Therefore, I am determined to do everything I can to stop you.

Lil' nigga, if it means that I have to kill you that is what I will do. He suddenly slammed on the breaks really hard making me hit the dash board.

He put the hand he had the gun in behind the seat pointing it at my back and said through his teeth "If I ever catch you in or around my house again, I will make you a homicide. Now get the fuck out of my car."

When I got out he sped off leaving me to have to walk back. I could tell this Samuel L. Jackson lookin muthafucka really meant what he said. He wasn't like anybody's Pastor that night but more like some old ass gangster.

I decided as I was taking that long walk back to town that I should probably respect him.

I told Sheila what happened and that I couldn't sneak into the house anymore. She said "Yup, that sounds like my daddy. Mama told me how he used to be and how she had to fight to turn him into the man he has come to be.

In many ways, you remind me of him. Maybe that's why I love you because I love him so much. He is everything to me."

I said "You knew this muthafucka was crazy and you had me sneaking in his house?" She said "Yes, but I never thought we would get caught and I certainly never knew he would use a gun to threaten to kill you!"

"Well, yeah, he did threaten to kill me and that muthafucka was serious" I said. She said "So it may be best if you didn't come over again." "Ya think!" I said.

Sheila laughed and said "Don't worry, I'll be getting my apartment soon. In the meantime, we can sneak… into… yo mama's… house" as she walked her fingers up my chest.

"What, no, you don't understand. My mama hates women; all women! If she caught us, that might be fatal for you! We'll just wait till you get your place." Sheila said "I'm gonna miss ya Poppi." I said "You gonna miss this dick." She yelled smiling "Shut up, nasty!"

****

Sheila had her baby, Raven Simone Johnson, two weeks before the beginning of her junior year in high school. With her mom's help and dad's support she was able to continue being an honors student while working to pay the bills for her apartment.

Lashaun, who is still living with his mom, also helped her out. He worked at a small restaurant in order to hide the real source of his money which he got from selling weed in a night club, gambling, and doing robberies with Mad Dog.

He told Sheila that he was working long hours in order to cover the time he was spending sexing up other women and his criminal activities with Mad Dog. However, at the start of their senior year in high school Lashaun's lies catch up with him. He is arrested and sentenced to 2 years in prison.

Chapter 3

D-BLOCK

"The primary obligation of any prisoner is to escape. Whether that means actually leaving or simply figuring out a way to handle things so you don't go crazy is up to you."
~ Emmanuel Goldstein

One of the drug boys in the hood was named Skillet. He was a really dark skinned cat with cracks in his skin from acne which reminded one of his boys of their grand mama's black skillet.

Skillet and his crew did business outside the Arab store on Courtland. These cats were mostly cool. We didn't bother them, they didn't bother us, and we kicked it with them every now and then.

Lately, Skillet had been driving this sweet supped up Chevy Monte Carlo with a candy apple red paint job, silver spoke rims, that was rolling on 20's, with large white wall tires. This joint was fast, loud and hot; a straight up chick magnet.

Mad Dog was excited about having one just like it himself one day. Out of the blue Skillet offers to let him rent it for the rest of the day. Only $300 and he could ride in style a while.

Mad Dog begged me to help him get the money. So we rolled over to a corner store on Northland and Scheule that was owned by some Vietnamese people. They were pretty easy to rob.

Plus, the police could barely understand what they were saying so it was hard for them to get a good enough description to catch us. We hit the store for $570 then went back to rent the car.

After paying Skillet he demanded that we have the car back by midnight or we'd have to pay another $300. He tossed Mad Dog a free bag of weed for us to get our head bad as we ride.

When I saw the bag had some stems and seeds I said "C'mom man. This is Reggie. I know you save this for the suckers. Give us a bag of that Loud."

I should have known something was up right then because his black ass chuckled and said "Awaight, you right dog."

Mad Dog and me had to look good for the honies so we dashed over to King City on Bailey to get some fresh gear. We both bought a pair of black jeans, white t-shirts and black NY Yankee's base ball caps with white stripes.

Not more than an hour into our joy ride we were kickin it with a couple of smoking hot honies in the McDonald's parking lot. Just then 3 police cars rolled up on us at full speed, pulled us out of the car, and had us cuffed before we knew it.

The thing Skillet forgot to tell us was that the car was a crack rental. The punk ass owner, who rented it out in return for free drugs, had reported it stolen. So, we got caught up in Skillet's bullshit and now we gonna wind up doin his bullet.

When the police walked us into the station house Mr. Tron, the Vietnamese man from the store we robbed, was there making a report. When he saw us being brought in he went crazy pointing at us and saying in his broken English "dat's deem, dat's deem!"

Not only are we arrested on stolen car charges, we get pinched on the robbery, and to make matters worse Mad Dog still had the gun on him.

They had locked us in separate rooms and before I knew what was happening Mad Dog had confessed to all the charges and told the cops that I had nothing to do with any of it. He told them that I was not with him during the robbery.

As, for me, I thought that shit was stupid so I wasn't confessing to nothing. In fact, I never said a thing except one word "lawyer".

In spite of my many requests for a lawyer the cops kept pressing me for hours trying to get me to make a statement. But every 30 minutes or so I would just look at them and say "lawyer".

Our trial date was set early and it was all over pretty quick. Mr. Tron showed up to testify, pointed us out as the robbers, and that was basically it.

After the police testified the Judge almost forced our attorney and the prosecutor to move to closing arguments. The jury deliberated for maybe 45 minutes and the verdict was "guilty".

The Judge immediately passed sentence: 12 years for Mad Dog due to his confession and gun possession and 5 years for me, 2 in prison and 3 on probation, for the robbery. The next thing I knew I was on the bus for Wende prison.

Wende Correctional Facility is a maximum security prison located outside of a little hick town called Alden in upstate NY. I was only 17 at the time, but a man by NY State standards, and could therefore be housed in prison with grown men.

They kept me segregated for a few days then assigned me to A-Block where they housed some of the nastiest looking niggas you ever want to see.

As I was being led into my cell these niggas stood up from the tables where they were playing their games and stared at me. I returned their stares trying to maintain an act of fearlessness... but I was scared. I had heard the stories about how these fools like to rape niggas.

I had made up my mind that if anybody tried to rape me they would have to fuck a corpse. I decided that I was not going to be alive while some 300 pound muthafucka was trying to dig a tunnel to Mexico through my asshole.

Day one in A-Block went by and everything is cool. I'm still getting the stares but nobody is fuckin with me. When we got released for rec on day two and everyone went out to the yard I decided to stay inside to shoot some hoops.

I had heard that some cats have even gotten raped out on the yard in broad daylight. So, I figured that I would simply stay out of sight as much as I could for the next few weeks until I could make some friends and/or buy protection.

I went to the gym equipment room to sign out a basketball. The cat at the desk brought the ball but quickly turned and walked away. I turned around quick to see what he just saw and standing there blocking the door was Monster and his crew.

Monster was that down-low homo cat who liked to target for rape handsome young men like me with smooth features. He approached me, with his crew in back of him, and said in a low growl "You are either going to give me some of that boy pussy or I'm gonna take it."

He wanted me to collapse like a bitch right in front of him. So I said "What are you some kind of big fuckin faggot". He said "I ain't no faggot, I likes pussy and you the closest thing I've seen to a bitch in a long time.

Now, you gonna give me some of that pussy or am I gonna have to take it?" I said "You might take it but you gonna take a ass whuppin with it".

Then I rushed Monster knowing that I only had seconds to put him down before his crew jumped in. I used my forehead to break the bridge of Monster's nose.

Even with a broken nose and bleeding heavily from the face Monster still raped me violently after his crew beat me mercilessly. I was hospitalized at ECMC for almost a month healing from internal injuries.

Around about 4 days left in my recovery they brought me back to the infirmary in Wende. I looked up from my bed that was one of 6 in the room and I saw this fine ass lady Corrections Officer (CO) walking by.

At first sight she reminded me of mama but she was really gorgeous! She went to the bed of another inmate, informed him that he would be assigned to her floor and explained to him that she wouldn't be taking any shit.

The man acted like being assigned to her floor was a blessing that just fell from heaven. She did kind of look like an angel and all but I was curious as what made the man so happy.

When she was about to pass by my bed walking out I said to her "Ma'am I'm new here can you answer a question for me?" She stopped and simply looked at me. She didn't say anything for about 20 seconds and then she said "Well!"

I said "Yes, I'm well" they are about to let me out of here. She must have thought my response was either dumb or funny because the corner of her mouth started to turn up in a smile. Then she composed herself and said "What is your question?"

****

This lady CO is Jasmine "Honey" Brown. Jasmine is a 35 year old very attractive Black, Italian and Cuban mixed woman who works the overnight shift and guards the 3rd Floor of D-Block.

She has an instant sexual attraction to Lashaun. Jasmine also has a secret passion for anal and oral sex. The anal she likes to get but the oral she loves to give. She confesses to her friends that giving oral sex makes her come. She says "sometimes I believe my G-spot is in the back of my throat."

Many men both outside and inside of Wende have tried to get Jasmine in bed and failed. Jasmine never lets a man choose her. She always chooses him in order to, in her mind, remain in the power position.

She has decided that she is going to choose Lashaun. She likes the way he looks, the way his lips move when he talks, and she has just got to have him.

****

I said "That man over there was so happy to be transferred to your block. What do I have to do to get transferred there? I can't have those punk ass goons in A-Block thinking they can jump on me whenever they get ready. I'm gonna wind up doing life in here

43

cause I'm gonna have to kill one of them to keep them off of me.

So what do I have to do to get transferred to a block where I can do my time quietly and get out of here as quick as possible?"

Once I stopped talking she stood there like a statue and just stared at me for another 20 seconds. Then she said "Why are you here?" Being a little irritated at the question I said "Cause I got beat the fuck up by some faggot ass punks." I didn't want to tell her that I was raped.

She said "No, why are you in prison?" I said "Oh, I thought you meant... I got caught up in a robbery with one of my boys." She asked "How much time you get?" "2 years with 3 on probation" I answered. Then she just stared at me again. I'm thinking in my mind, what is up with this crazy bitch?

She started walking away and said "I'm not making any promises. Let me see what my boss says." I said "Thanks Miss." She stopped, whirled around and gave me an evil look. Then I quickly said "I mean, Officer! Thanks Officer!" She turned again and left.

****

Jasmine stopped at the Nurse's Station to see if she could get information on Lashaun's injuries. The nurse told her that he suffered a fractured jaw, fractured arm, 3 cracked ribs and a ruptured spleen. Then she whispered "He was raped pretty bad too."

Just then Jasmine saw his date of birth on the nurse's chart and realized that Lashaun, who looks like he is in his twenties, is only 17. She immediately started to feel sorry for him and wanted to protect him.

She also had a thought in the back of her mind of how fine he is and how it could be easier to control a sexual situation in prison with a younger inmate. She was making herself excited just thinking about it.

Jasmine knew that she had a bed available on her floor but had to get permission from the Sergeant to move him.

Jack Shaffer, a Corrections Sergeant of 28 years, is in charge of the block. He has the authority for moving inmates and changing assignments within his block.

Jack has a secret obsession for Jasmine. He wants her so bad that she is all that he can think about sometimes. Jack was so obsessed that he would go out at night, leaving his wife and 4 children home alone, to stalk her from time to time.

He wanted to know who she was with and when. So he would sit outside of her house to see if he could catch a glimpse of her through the windows. He would only drive away and head back home after he saw her bedroom light go out.

Jack gives any man a hard time who gives Jasmine a hard time. He develops a hatred for and finds a reason to reassign any man who he thinks she might like or who she may give a little too much attention to.

Jasmine knows that Jack likes her but is unaware of the extent of his obsession. So she decided to use her feminine charms to get Lashaun transferred to her floor.

"Sergeant Shaaaaaffer" she calls out as she walks down the hall approaching his office door. "Whaaaaat" Shaffer replies. "What kind of trouble are you going to get me into now Officer Brown?"

"Who? Me? I would never get my favorite Sergeant in trouble", she laughs. "So what can I do for you then" Jack says smiling just happy to be in her presence.

There is this 17 year old kid who is about to be released from the infirmary. Some goons in A-Block beat him the fuck up, broke several of his bones, gave him internal injuries and raped the shit out of him."

"Yeah, I can imagine a lot of shit came out of him" Shaffer chuckled. Jasmine said "I know that he is basically a piece of shit, which is the reason why he is in prison, but he is just 17 and is only here to do 2 years. He doesn't need a group of grown ass men raping him every time he turns around. Shaffer laughs "Every time he turns around... you are funny!"

Jasmine says "Come on Jack, I'm not trying to be funny. This is serious. Let's find a way to do SOME good in this fuckin' place or at least TRY to help one person if we can."

Jack says "Ok, Ok, I see you are serious. Who is this kid?" "Lashaun Johnson. He is here on a 2 year robbery bid. I talked to him earlier and he is the type of kid, although he did commit a felony, who really shouldn't be in here with these killers."

Jack pulled up Lashaun's file on the computer as Jasmine was talking and says "You're right." "I will give him a chance but you have to make him know that if he causes any trouble in my block, I will bounce his ass back to A-Block dressed in a pink halter top and a tutu."

Jasmine laughed "You're sick Jack, but thanks." "Yeah, Yeah" Jack says. Jasmine leaves the office happy that she has conquered the male species once again.

****

The day before I was to be released from the infirmary I was laying in bed just about to doze off. Jasmine came to the foot of my bed and yelled "Inmate!" She scared the shit out of me. I jumped but once I saw who it was I said "Oh, yes Officer."

"Do you plan on being a problem?" she asked. "No ma'am" I said. She gave me that crazy fuckin stare again. Then she said "You are only getting one chance. No second chances. No reminders. No excuses. And nobody is going to feel sorry for you. You fuck up once and you are going back to A-Block. Do you understand?"

"Yes, ma'am" I said trying to contain my joy. "Good. I'm not in the habit of repeating myself. So, if you fuck up, you will look up and find yourself out of my block before you know what happened. Are we clear?" "Yes ma'am. Thank you, ma'am!" She gave me only a short stare this time before turning and walking away.

Now, just like the cat before who she told was going to her floor I was happier than a faggot with a bag of dicks!

You see, I talked to the man after Jasmine left that day to see why he was so happy to be transferred to D-Block. I mean, I was happy that Monster and his boys wouldn't have another chance to ream me in my ass or try to make me their bitch. But D-Block is one of the best assignments in the prison.

The Mess Hall is in D-Block. The Mess Hall is one of the best jobs in the prison and most of the inmates who live in D-Block work there. Jasmine got me a job working there too.

You have access to all the food, which reduces your need for commissary because you get the opportunity to smuggle some out for snacks late at night.

The only problem is inmates from the other blocks know that D-Block inmates work the Mess Hall and can smuggle food. So gang members from other blocks try to identify the weak D-Block inmates to make them become their food suppliers.

Once I started working there now here comes this Monster muthafucka and his crew fucking with me again. He sent one of the inmates who lived in D-Block with a message that he planned to punk me for extra food. He had it in mind to tax me two loaves of bread each day to keep his dick out of my ass.

I really had to think about what I was going to do because in prison food is power. I asked myself "Do I want to give this bitch anymore power over me or anybody else?"

You see, when inmates have no commissary a little extra food each day goes a long way. Most people know how cigarettes are traded for goods and services in prison but few know that food is currency too.

Delivering a couple slices of bread when an inmate is hungry at night can buy you a lot of favor, and a certain amount of power, in a prison.

After thinking about it for a while, I didn't want to give this nigga any more power especially not over me. So, I decided to join the Latin Kings for protection.

Not many other gangs messed with the Latin Kings because they had a reputation for being sick demented killers who never quit. If you fucked with them, they never stopped trying to get you back.

They never gave up and always took it a step further. If you shanked one of theirs, they would kill one of yours.

49

Once I joined the Kings that was it. Monster and his boys may have had me scared and runnin like a rabbit before but now the Latin Kings is my gun. "Ain't no fun when the rabbit's got a gun!" Fuck with me now you faggot ass bitch!

I'd rather put in work for my brothers, supplying them with extra food and getting respect, rather than having to pay some monkey lookin homo muthafucka to keep him off my ass.

The leader of the Latin Kings at the time was Victor Baudilio de Jesus aka Smiley. He earned the nick name Smiley because he was a crazy killer who had a habit of smiling and even laughing while he was viciously murdering a mug.

Smiley had moved his drug operation with Cali Cartel connections from California to New York. After a few years of being on top of the game in the Buffalo area he and 38 of his boys, along with 5 women, all got pinched in a multi-national FBI/DEA sting.

They put King Pin status on him which means that he is never getting out of prison. So there was nothing he wouldn't do or no murder he wouldn't commit to maintain his reputation and power in the prison. Nobody fucked with him.

Smiley took a liking to me and made me kind of his gang's mascot. I didn't mind because that meant that now nobody fucked with me either.

I could go anywhere I wanted to now without fear. I had a little power now but I was smart enough not to go around flexing cause muthafuckas would shank you just for that.

So, I used my power to go anywhere and do anything I wanted. I could go out on the yard or to the gym, with my brothers around of course, and not have to worry about anything too much. We worked out slinging the weights every day and I was able to get in and stay in good fighting shape.

The only thing about working out like that is my testosterone level was always high and so was my sex drive. I was choking the shit out of my dick almost every night. I was getting tired of jerkin off and needed some pussy real bad.

One night, after count time, Jasmine ordered me out of my cell to mop up water from a sink that she had let overflow in the mop closet. As I grabbed the mop she yelled "that mop stinks, get a new mop head from the supply closet."

When I entered the closet she went in behind me and shut the door. I said "What the hell are you doing" and she said "shut up and kiss me muthafucka".

"Oh, shit! This is just what the doctor ordered" I said to myself. I gave her a long passionate kiss. She pulled down my pants and took a long passionate suck on my dick. It was so good cause I hadn't had no pussy or a good blow job in so long that I came quickly.

I thought she might get mad like some bitches do when you come to quick but she just kept on sucking, and licking, and tugging, and sucking until it rose back up. She really made love to my dick; sucking and pulling on it so good until I came again. Damn that was good and just what I needed!

Her passionate sucking and the two intense orgasms she gave me while standing up the whole time made me weak and slightly dizzy. Man, I had never had it like that before.

She led me back to my bed and locked me in my cell. She told me later that after she put me to bed she went back to her desk and discretely pleasured herself with a finger vibrator while fantasizing that I was inside of her.

From then on, two or three times a week, deep into the night, while everyone was sleep Jasmine would find an excuse to let me out of my cell so we could have supply room sex.

That is when I found out that this fine muthafucka was a freak who liked taking dick in the ass. During these brief but intense sessions Jasmine sometimes had to beg me to fuck her anally cause I wasn't really into it. But I did it just to keep getting that pussy and my dick sucked.

Jasmine liked to get hit hard, fast and deep. As I would thrust hard and burry my dick as quickly and deeply as I could over and over, making it disappear between her big round pancake brown butt cheeks, she would pound into her pussy a large ribbed rubber dildo while massaging her clit.

This led both of us to some of the quickest and most intense orgasms either of us had ever had in our lives. Jasmine often had to stuff her mouth with towels to muffle the screams she couldn't help making as we delivered each other intense orgasmic pleasure.

I was hooked on that pussy and Jasmine was hooked on my dick to the point where she was ready to risk everything to keep getting it as much as possible.

****

A certified redneck country cowboy CO, Cleon "Bubba" Casey, had a thing for Jasmine. Bubba hates Black men but creams his pants at the simple thought of fucking a black woman.

He really likes Jasmine in particular. He wants her more than the lungs want air when they can't get it and has often thought of raping her.

Bubba is called "The Mayor of Hillbilly Hamlet" by Black inmates because the 1st floor inmates that he guards are all white country boys like himself. He has no problem saying openly "I ain't baby sittin no niggers."

Bubba works the day shift but volunteers for overtime at night so he can be there while Jasmine is working. He periodically leaves his floor unguarded so that he can sneak upstairs just to get a look at or have a brief conversation with her.

****

One night Bubba saw Jasmine acting too friendly with me while letting me back into my cell after one of our sex sessions. This made him angry, jealous and suspicious even after she angrily denied his suspicions.

But this redneck bastard saw something he didn't like and now he began to do everything he could to screw with me. He was determined to make my life miserable so that I might make a request to leave or force me to be transferred to another Block.

He would do things like sneak behind my cell on the cat walk and turn off the water or damage the pipes so that I would be unable to wash or flush for a few days.

Inmates can only take showers or make phone calls once or twice a week. Bubba made sure other CO's skipped me for my shower or my turn to use the phone on days or times when Jasmine wasn't there. He would also do things like cut the power to my cell so that I would have to sit in the dark for days at a time.

On days when I had a visitor Bubba sometimes volunteered to be the visiting room officer. He especially liked to harass Sheila when she came to visit just to make me angry.

Sheila would dress a little sexy for her visits to give me something to look at and look forward to coming home for. Bubba would make her sit at a table facing him at the desk and then make comments like "Look at'em big brown ballons."

As I walked into the room he would say stupid shit like "Somebody else gon be licken on nem titties ta nite boy." I learned to just ignore that muthafucka. He didn't know I could have easily killed him.

Even though he fucked with me regularly I never felt like he had power over me. To me he was just was a powerless punk who did cowardly punk ass shit that punk ass pussies do just because they can.

Once visits ended, inmates were stripped searched to ensure no contraband was passed to them. Bubba loved to be in the room while I was being searched. He would make comments like "Oooo, look at the size of that asshole. I can tell a lot of dicks been up in there!"

Bubba did everything he could to provoke me into a fight in his dogged effort to force me to be transferred to another block. I kept my cool and took all of his bullshit. I refused to let that punk ass inbred redneck bastard win.

Shelia was still holding on to the ideal of me and her being married and raising a family together so she visited me as much as she could. But she wasn't used to anybody funkin with her.

She had a hard time handling the attitude and harassment she got from the CO's. Her breasts were still large and heavy from breast feeding so she made the mistake of wearing an underwire bra to the prison.

They took her into a room and made her take it off, watched while she undressed, and gave it back to her in a bag when she left. She had never felt so humiliated in her life.

On each visit she had to get body searched which she hated. The thing she hated the most was all the sexual harassment she got from Bubba. Sheila finally had had enough and exploded.

She angrily told me one day that this would be her last visit. Sheila was my first love so I didn't want to let her go and I didn't expect her to give up on me. I looked forward to her visits because they helped me to maintain my sanity and to be able to put up with all the prison bullshit.

When Sheila told me that she wasn't going to visit anymore I lost it. Before I realized what I was doing I exploded. I stood up and yelled "You gonna abandon me bitch!"

The officers tried to make me calm down but I was angry so I wouldn't calm down. Eventually they had to take me down to keep me from getting to Sheila as she walked out crying.

Me and Jasmine continued to have our secret sex sessions for the next 18 months. That is, until one day while she laid on her back with me on top trying to dig out the back of that pussy, Jasmine, thinking it might intensify my pleasure, penetrated my ass with the dildo. I freaked out and briefly but viscously beat her.

I stormed out of the closet and locked myself back in my cell. Now I couldn't sleep that night because I know that I fucked up but I don't know what's gonna happen next. I kept hearing Jasmine's voice in my head echoing the threat of being bounced back to A-Block.

Jasmine couldn't tell anyone what actually happened without ruining herself. So she had to claim that she slipped and fell down the stairwell to cover her injuries. But our sexual encounters ended and I was paroled six weeks later.

After a being out of Wende almost 3 years, I saw Monster riding in a vintage 1976 green Cadillac Eldorado Convertible with white leather interior.

He was drinking Crystal from the bottle and sharing a blunt with two nice looking ladies. One of them was a really fine red bone with a big ass afro and wearing giant hoop earrings.

I watched as Monster pulled into a McDonald's parking lot off E. Delavan and I began tracking his every move. As he was getting out of the car the red bone must have said something that he didn't like.

He grabbed her by the neck, growled something at her close to her face, and snatched her by her afro hair which came off in his hand. It was a wig. He laughed and threw it in the back seat.

As soon as Monster went in McDonald's he stepped into the bathroom. The bathroom in lock up was always a good place to shank a fool. I figured this is my chance to get him good.

I snuck up behind him and quickly stabbed him in the back of the neck just below the base of his skull. This was a move to take a big muthafucka down quick that I learned from Smiley.

The point of this type of cut is to sever the brain stem, take a fool off his feet, and take away his air or ability to breathe. No air, no feet, no fight.

The cut worked well just like Smiley said it would because it paralyzed Monster instantly. He got a violent case of the shakes but the cut didn't kill him right away.

He was making some sounds so I punched him in the face as hard as I could to try to knock him out. As I hit him I said "Who's the punk now bitch!" I only succeeded in breaking two of my knuckles. He was still lying on the floor looking at me but shaking like a fuckin break dancer.

I knew I couldn't leave this muthafucka only half dead so I drug him to the toilet, stuck his head in the bowl, and held him down until he drowned. Once he stopped shaking I knew he was gone.

I pulled his pants down and sat him up on the toilet so it would look like he was just in there taking a shit. Then I went to the counter and ordered two Big Macs from the Dollar Menu and a root beer to go.

Just as I got my order somebody discovered Monster was dead and chaos broke out in the store. But I calmly walked away almost unnoticed by all the people who were now gathering around there.

I said to myself after taking a long sip on my soda "No more boy pussy for you muthafucka!"

Chapter 4

LANEESHA

"True love is like a pair of socks;
you gotta have two and they've gotta match."
~ Keith Sweat

Laneesha Barnes is a straight up ratchet chick. But she is that ride-or-die kind of bitch that is always looking out and trying to be down with a nigga watching his back. One of her favorite sayings was "I'm a true bitch" meaning that she was always faithful. After Mad Dog she became my robber partner and gun carrying wheel woman.

I first met Laneesha in a afterhours gambling joint on E. Delavan. It was upstairs in the back over an Arab store where they also had underage strippers. I sold about $100 in weed every night and won sometimes up to $700 playing Black Jack and another card game called Tunk.

Mama's husband Leroy had taught me some things about how to win at card games and I became good at it. "One of the tricks, he said, is never play a game that doesn't give you the opportunity to cheat every now and then.

When gambling the odds are stacked against you so you have to learn how to lower the odds. Cheating pigeons, not experienced gamblers (that will get you killed), is how you lower the odds and win big."

He also taught me about the psychology of winning. He said "Most people are losers and they know it. They gamble hoping to win but they expect to lose. Life is a game of expectations.

A woman has a baby because she is expecting to have one. She goes out and buys clothes, cribs and all that shit before the baby gets here because she's expecting and therefore she gets a baby.

Winners win because they expect to win. When people recognize you as a winner, they expect to lose to you so they do. You can cheat they ass all night and no one will suspect you because they expect you to win.

Plus, a scared man never wins. Most men are so scared they are going to lose that they do. Never gamble with anything you can't afford to lose."

I followed his strategy to a T became a winner at gambling. I often won because people expected me to win. I never shot dice because it was too hard to cheat good enough to lower the odds.

So once in a while when I saw the betting had stopped because somebody was on a hot streak and the pot was big, I would just walk in the room and yell "What's the bet?"

Whatever it was I didn't care because I would hear the gasps when I walked in there. Almost every time I walked out with the pot once the shooter became scared because people expected me to win.

I used to see Laneesha in the joint a lot but never really said anything to her but hi. She was that loud, ghetto, tattoo on the neck kind of chick that liked to have fun.

Laneesha was about 5'3" weighing 115 pounds with a short Halle Berry type hair cut, almond colored skin, and a nice little booty to be so skinny. She kind of reminds you of Cherrelle. I started thinking to myself "She might be a little hottie!"

Just as I had that thought, I see two cats come in setting up to rob the joint. One positioned himself in a corner near me behind Laneesha and the other one went to the bar.

As soon as the one at the bar pulled out a shot gun and raised it in the air, Laneesha whipped out a .25 auto, I don't know from where, and POW, shot that muthafucka in the side of the head.

I knew nigga #2 was about to make a move so I quickly grabbed a champagne bottle off the table and smashed it across his forehead.

When he fell forward his head hit Laneesha in the back of the head and knocked her out. It was chaos in the place so I picked Laneesha up, threw her over my shoulder, grabbed her gun and dashed out.

I forced a cat out of his car at gun point, dropped Laneesha in and ducked into a little seedy motel on Main and High Street.

She had a big ass knot on the back of her head. So I laid her on the bed face down, put some ice in a towel, and held it against her head. She was breathing and everything ok so I covered her up and let her sleep. I slept in the chair.

We both woke up at the same time. She looked around and said "What the fuck? How did I get here?" I told her what happened and handed her the gun. She said "I got to get outta here" and tried to stand up but fell back down on the bed dizzy.

I told her "You need to rest some more and eat." There was a McDonald's and Burger King down the street so I went and got us 2 big pancake breakfasts, orange juice, water and milk.

She ate but threw it all back up. I had seen cats on the football team do the same thing after getting hit in the head so I figured she had a concussion.

I didn't want to use that stolen car anymore. Since we were close to Buffalo General Hospital I walked her over there. We told them a tree branch had fallen and struck her in the head so they wouldn't think a crime had been committed and call the cops.

After finding out that she was basically ok, she took the medication they gave her and slept the rest of the day. I went to sleep again too and when I woke up she was already awake staring at me.

I said "Hey, you're awake." She asked suspiciously "Why did you take care of me?" I said "I don't know. It seemed like the right thing to do. Besides, I couldn't leave you knocked out in that joint and let the cops catch you."

"Hmmm" she responded. Then she pulled up the covers and looked down at her pussy and said "You didn't fuck me did you?" I laughed and said "No, if I fucked you that shit would still be smokin."

She said "Well, if you didn't take none I owe you some." We hit it gently because her head still hurt some but it was good.

As we laid there together I asked her if she remembered what happened last night because I was curious about why she went gangsta on them niggas. She said "I shot this muthafucka then things went black."

I filled in the rest of the story for her and then I asked "Why did you shoot him?" She said "It was my job. I was working security." I sat up and looked at her little ass and said "Security?"

She said "What, nigga, you surprised a bitch can handle herself?" I said "No but I never would have suspected..." "That's the point, she said, nobody would have suspected. We knew sooner or later somebody was gonna try to hit the joint and we wanted to giv'em a nice surprise."

We started sharing the stories of our lives and she hit me with another bomb.

She told me how her stepfather started raping her when she was 10. She told her mother but her mother didn't believe her.

By age 12 she had gotten tired of this muthafucka getting drunk, coming in her room, and trying to make her suck his dick and her mother not trying to protect her. So she made a plan to make her mother and him pay.

She knew where he hid his gun and that he kept gasoline in the garage. Her mom had recently been receiving threatening phone calls from an ex-con ex-husband who she divorced while he was in prison. This was the right time to execute her plan because the focus would be on him.

Laneesha shot both of them 3 times each as they slept, doused them with gas, and set them on fire. She stayed in the house as it burned figuring the neighbors would call the fire department.

She wanted the firefighters to bring her out so they would see her as a rescued victim. And she laughed when telling me about how she put on a big act for them and the police crying for her mommy. From then on, she was my back havin boo and we was tight like glue.

Chapter 5

LOLA

"I would rather my enemy's sword pierce
my heart then my friend's dagger
stab me in the back."
~ Michele Bardsley

Lola Braxton was a Licensed Practical Nurse. She was an attractive 23 year old Black woman with clear beautiful skin the color of milk chocolate. Her breasts are 32 B, waist is 23; she had big pretty lips with 40 inch hips.

She stood 5 feet 2 inches tall weighing 130 pounds but 35 of those pounds are all ass. She was the type of lady whose figure snaps right back after having a baby.

This girl was built like a cross between R2D2 and a Shetland pony. She was short and solid like a fire hydrant with a powerful booty that looked like the backside of a little horse.

Lola was very intelligent but not very smart when it came to picking men. She had a pattern of choosing one abuser after another to be in relationship with. Although she was super attractive Lola did not feel beautiful because the men in her life had beaten her down mentally and emotionally. She suffered therefore from low self esteem.

Lola did not feel worthy to have the type of man she really wanted so she chose the men who really wanted her. As a result, she would end up with one abusive man after another.

Lola had three children: a set of 5 year old twin girls and a boy that is 2. Both of her baby's fathers are abusive men who used the children to continue to gain access to and torment her.

There were two young men that Lola dated between her baby's daddies who also abused her physically and emotionally. The thing about Lola was she didn't just fold up and take the abuse. She did try to fight back.

She had a permanent restraining order against the twin's father. He was currently in prison serving time on felony contempt of court charges for violating the judge's order to stay away from her.

Lola met this man who was 33 the summer she turned 17. She had already graduated high school and had a full scholarship to Vanderbilt School of Nursing.

This cat made her believe that she didn't need college to help him in the music producing business that he was planning to start. She believed him because she thought that she was so in love with him. She thought that he loved her as much as she loved him because he made her feel special.

Lola ran away from the very nice, comfortable, upper middle-class home that her mom provided her to be with this cat. Yet, he had her living in a vacant house at one point where he was stealing electricity from next door.

He purposely got her pregnant and convinced her to marry him when she was 18 in order to stop her mother from trying to rescue her. Lola was now his wife so there was nothing more her mother could do to stop him.

Through his violent and abusive actions, though, he stopped himself. Criminal court proceedings forced him to have to leave Lola alone.

He is doing 19 years in Attica because, in addition to contempt of court, he was also convicted on other felony charges of criminal mischief, burglary and aggravated assault for kicking in her door, entering her home and beating her severely.

Even from prison he used his mother, on the pretence of wanting to see his children, to continue to torment her.

Like many abused women Lola made the mistake of trusting the woman who gave birth to the monster: his mother.

Abusers' mothers act like their only interest is in the grand children. In reality, they sometimes assist their abusive boys in gaining access to and help providing opportunities for them to continue to abuse their victims.

Lola ultimately had to get family, friends and other parties included in the restraining order in order to finally end her twin's father reign of terror on her.

You see, many mothers of abusive men are in denial that they gave birth to a monster. Their first reaction is to always defend them.

They are inclined to blame the victim saying things like their sons always choose the wrong women. So they support their sons in their abuse deceiving themselves into believing that their victims are crazy or had some other problem.

They don't want to recognize however that a man couldn't stand over and stomp a mud hole in another woman unless he truly hated his mother. He may continuously dote on his mom, giving the impression that he really loves her in order to manipulate her to keep helping him, but the reality is he actually hates her.

There are other mothers of abusive men who know that their sons, while adult size, are just man sized boys. They don't want these big babies living in their house so they push the responsibility for finishing raising them onto another woman.

Yet, each time the woman who mama pushed them on kicks the big boy out, they come running back to mama's house.

This type of mother always tries to act like she is on the victim's side. She rushes to the victim's house to intervene and make peace after her son has an angry outburst and beats the victim up or breaks everything in her house.

This mother's goal is to get the victim to keep dealing with her big baby so she won't have to take him back into her house.

Neither of these types of abusive mothers or grandmothers is good for the victims of their abusive sons to communicate with. The abuser keeps tabs on his victim through his mother.

Therefore, the mother/grandmother has to be cut off also. Lola has wised up now and cut off both of her abusers and their mothers. She feels like she is at the beginning of turning her life around when she meets Lashaun. However, she is unaware that he is another style of but just as much of an abuser as any other.

****

The hand that I broke on Monster's face was now swollen twice its normal size. It is throbbing and hurting more than I can take. I thought it might just be sore and would heal on its own after a while. But now I know that was wrong and I need to get help.

I went to ECMC's emergency room and waited about two hours to be seen. I got a little agitated because it took so long to get into an examining room.

Now I've been back here about a half hour before the doctor comes in. He looked at my hand all of 6 seconds and asked "What happened here?"

I said "A friend and I watched a karate movie and decided that we could break boards. I know. It was stupid."

He tried to straighten my fingers out and saw that it caused me pain. He said "I need to order some X-rays" and just walked out of the room. "Muthafucka" I said to myself.

A person who normally mops the floors or something took me over to the X-ray Department. I sat there another 20 minutes before the X-ray Tech came in.

He pissed me off too because he had to work and twist my hand around in different painful positions in order to get the angles the doctor wanted. I went back to the examining room and waited another half hour before the nurse came in.

By this time I've laid back on the bed trying to calm myself because I was steaming mad. When the door opened and the nurse walked in all my anger was gone.

I saw this fine ass muthafucka with a big beaming smile coming through the door. She said "Sorry for the wait Mr. Johnson. I'm nurse Braxton and I will be taking care of you today..."

The rest of what she said was like background noise because I was looking at her gorgeous face with those big pretty lips and those wide ass hips. I started to imagine myself hittin that right there.

"Mr. Johnson…, Mr. Johnson are you ok?" "Oh, yes" I said. "Excuse me, my mind drifted off for a second. What is your name again?"

"I'm Nurse Braxton. The doctor has determined that you have fractured your hand in two places. You will need to be prepped for a cast. I will be right back and we will get started."

When she walked out of the room, her butt cheeks were moving in those hospital pants like two midgets wresting in a pillow case. Not only was she fine, this heffa was hot too. She had this thing about her that was just sexy. Man, I had to get me some of that.

When she came back in the room, she had a tray with a needle on it. Then she asked me playfully "I see you looking at the needle. Are you going to be a baby or big boy?" "I'll be a big boy if you let me be your baby" I said.

Surprisingly, she looked me in my eyes and smiled kind of sexy like, tenderly grabbed my hand, and said "It's a deal." Before I knew it she hit me with that needle right in the area where I knew it was broken. It hurt but I didn't want to flinch too much.

She said "Now, that's a big boy" patted me on my thigh, grabbed the tray and walked back out of the room. Each time I got to see her walk away it was like a lusty little treat for me. Ooooo, she was fine.

Ten minutes later she came back in the room with everything she needed to make a cast. She said "Your hand should be rather numb now so this shouldn't hurt too much."

I had to get a date with this lady. I wanted her to know that I was interested without seeming creepy and getting cut off too quick.

I started asking her about why she chose nursing as a profession. I told her how I was mad for having to wait so long in pain and how her presence took all the anger away. I complemented her on the tender way she was applying the cast.

Then, I wanted to touch on her sense of spirituality if she had any, and told her that it seemed to me that nursing might be her godly gift or calling. I told her how I had been waiting for GOD to show me the right woman because I was ready to settle down and have a family.

Once I saw that caught her interest I said "There is a Tim Horton's downstairs in the lobby, do you think we could meet tomorrow briefly for coffee or tea?"

Her eyes looked into mine deeply for a few seconds and then she said "Sure, Mr. Johnson, why not? Would Noon be ok for you?" I said "I'll be there."

We had a good time talking, laughing and getting to know each other. Within two weeks I was bouncing off that big pretty ass like a kid playing in a bouncy house. She had some good ass pussy too.

Her body was so tight I couldn't believe she had three kids. Most women with three children have stretch marks and their stomachs look like crumpled up paper. Lola's skin was smooth and a pretty chocolate brown almost without a blemish.

I really loved making love to Lola and she really loved being made love to. Sheila was a sexy woman too but Lola is very sexy and feminine in a way that is hard to describe.

The way that she becomes soft and sinks her body into mine as she lay in my arms is super feminine. It just feels really good simply holding her.

One Sunday, we were lying on the couch together watching a movie and I noticed Lola's cell phone kept pinging over and over that she was receiving text messages. Then, it started ringing back to back, over and over.

I asked her who is calling and texting her like that and she said "My son's father". I said to myself, oh hell no, and answered the phone when he called again.

"Hello, be a man and tell me your name muthafucka" I said. "My name is killer Conway and you are gonna be dead by the next day if you don't get yo ass outta my house to day" he said and hung up.

I turned off the TV, moved her feet off the couch and made her sit up. I looked her in the eye and told her "Listen, I've been in situations like this before where a woman is being stalked and abused. Nobody can help her because she is too scared to give anybody any information about the nigga.

Are you going to be too scared too or are you going to let me help you make this muthafucka stop bothering you?"

She looked at me a minute and then said "His name is Kevin Conway, he lives on Rommel St off Broadway, he drives a black BMW with CONWAY on the plates, and likes to hang at Jazzy's on Genesee.

I kissed her on the forehead and said "That's all I need to know" then left.

I went and got my lil' ride-or-die bitch Laneesha for back up and rolled up to Jazzy's to see if he was there. Sure enough the BMW is parked out front.

I had Laneesha go into the club to see how many people where in there, who he was with, and to kick his car on the way to set his alarm off.

When she went in she yelled somebody is messing with a black BMW outside. He came out and looked around to see if anyone was around and reset the alarm.

I looked at this nigga and he looked very familiar. I knew that I knew him from somewhere but couldn't place him. I was racking my brain trying to figure it out because I knew that I knew this nigga.

Suddenly, I knew exactly who this muthafucka was. He was the bitch that stole mama's meat from me. I couldn't believe it!

I had vowed to get this muthafucka one day and here was my chance. I was so psyched that events had worked out this way.

This wasn't about Lola anymore. Now I wanted to take this nigga out in the worse way as revenge for stealing my mama's meat.

I learned from Smiley that if you are going to kill a muthafucka it has to be up close and personal. Otherwise, you could leave a fool only half dead and he may end up a witness against you.

He also taught me that if you use a gun it is best to use a long barrel revolver because it has more power and you won't leave casings at the scene. Also, with a long barrel it is easier to attach a homemade silencer. A hollowed out potato is a good one but the best is a 2 liter pop bottle taped to the barrel.

For this job I chose to use the bottle and a .357 magnum. I kicked his car again and waited on the side of the building. When he came out I put one in the back of his head. I didn't expect it to explode like a busted watermelon but it did and that was the end of him.

I said "That's for stealing my mama's meat muthafucka" and walked off. Me and Laneesha laughed half the night about him dying for stealing my mama's meat. She was crazy and crazy funny too.

About six weeks after the funeral of her son's father Lola asked me to move in with her. I told her that I had a job but the truth is I had started moving crack and heroine for this mid-level baller: Sly Davis.

I was also selling dime bags of MJ as my side hustle and every now and then would do a robbery with Laneesha. I needed a nice cushy place to stay so I am down.

In order to pull this off though, I worked the corners from 7 in the morning and post up at the rock house till it's time to break out at 6 in the evening. I would come home to Lola in the evening to make it look like I was doing factory work.

She is happy, I'm happy. She feeds me, bathes me, takes care of my clothes and makes sure that I get plenty of that pussy.

Laneesha thinks that she is my woman. In order to keep her working to back me up I have to half way break my dick off in her ass every now in then. This girl is crazy but controllable.

She told me that if a man doesn't beat her ass every now and then to keep her in line, he's a punk. So, from time to time I have to go up side her head when it looked like she was crusin' for a brusin'. For whatever reason, this turned her on and she liked me to bust in her ass after I beat her ass.

Now, the way Laneesha liked to have sex I call it "monkey fuckin". She liked to get into acrobatic shit where she wanted me to do things like hold her on my shoulder so she could suck my dick while hanging upside down.

She is petit so she was easy to handle but this little muthafucka was a high energy fuck. You had to be in shape to mess with her. The trick is to make her do all the work while ordering her around like a director on a movie set. She liked that shit.

One of her favorite positions was having me stand against the wall. She would hop up, clasp her hands behind my neck, put her feet on the wall, and just pump on my dick like a monkey swinging on a pole. It was fun fuckin her but this crazy bitch will wear you out if you let her.

Things started going downhill with me and Lola after I called her Laneesha one day while we were fuckin'. She came up with the idea to do some different things to "spice up" the sex. So she started doing some monkeyfied shit that reminded me of Laneesha and before I knew it I was talking to her, while busting that ass, like I talk to Laneesha.

Of course, she was hotter than fish grease. I tried to play it off but she was too smart for that bullshit because she had heard it all before with the other men who had been in her life.

She was yelling in my face and talking so much shit that before I knew it I smacked her hard across the face and said "Shut up about that bullshit bitch, damn!"

Now, she was no longer feeling safe with me and things started to change. The trust was gone and she began to watch my every move.

I knew it was just a matter of time before I would have to leave Lola. But I had invested a lot of my money into taking care of her home and her kids. I was going to need quick cash to make the exit plus I wanted to upgrade my living status.

I had 10k to invest in product but Sly wouldn't deal for that small amount. He told me that I could put up the 10k as a down payment on 100k weight and gave me 4 months to roll his end back to him.

I thought to myself, damn, this is just the type of deal I needed right now. Man, I felt blessed and was ready to rock. I had my girl Lanessha who would work around the clock if I needed her to.

The only thing I didn't have was a safe place to stash the product. Lola and her kids rarely went into their basement so I decided to hide it there. I figured I could hold on with her another 4 months and then be out.

The problem with the plan is the extra weight brought extra traffic which brought attention from the feds. They had actually been watching Sly and tried unsuccessfully to catch him on phone taps.

After I made my transaction with him they got up on me too. They had been following me and knew that I was living with Lola. They planned to pop me and then use me as an informant against Sly and as a front to make their drug buys. They wanted to get some of our transactions on tape.

The way that I found this out is they raided Lola's house while she and I were sleeping at 2 AM one Wednesday morning.

This was the story they told me but it was all bullshit. It did not make sense to me that they knew Sly was my supplier and knew about our transaction but didn't get any of it on tape. Get the fuck outta here with that shit! Nah muthafucka, I smelled a rat and it was Lola.

After she stopped trusting me, she hired a private investigator to follow me to see what I was doing and with who. He told her all about my drug activity and that I had my stash in her basement.

This muthafucka advised her to call the FBI so that she wouldn't get caught up in my shit. That is exactly what this bitch did too. The FBI set up the raid with her help and got my money along with my stash.

Now I am fucked in more ways than one. Not only am I arrested and broke but I'm also 90 thousand dollars in debt. Sly is not going to care that the feds got my stash. He is still going to want his money.

I was so mad at Lola I couldn't see straight. If it is the last thing I do, I am going to fuck this bitch up. I was good to this muthafucka and she turned on me like that. She was going to have to pay.

The feds didn't really have a federal drug case against me so they turned me over to the County Sherriff and processed me into the Erie County Holding Center.

The second day there I ran into this crazy ass Indian who figured out a way to escape through the air ducts. In the first floor hallway, they kept bins with outside clothing of the inmates that were about to be released. I stole some clothes and prepared to escape with the Indian.

Then one of the Deputies came and told me to get ready to move out. At first I was confused and didn't know if they found out about the plan or what so I just did what I was told.

They gave me my discharge papers, my property, and I was out. It turned out that these clowns had mistakenly discharged me like they had done with many others over the years. Anyway, I was free and I was determined that nobody was going to find me.

The first thing I did was go to Lola's house so that I could catch her by surprise before the word of my escape got out.

When I snuck into the house this muthafucka was taking a bath and singing. I thought to myself, I know why the caged bird sings: because the bitch is a snitch!

I knew that she liked to lay in the tub until she fell asleep so I got a butcher knife from the kitchen and waited until she dozed off.

When I saw her head sink down and she made that little lady snore, I pounced and hit her in the neck two times hard and deep. On the second strike I hit her like I hit Monster. Instead of shaking like crazy it was over for her in a second but she was bleeding like crazy.

I pulled the plug on the tub to let the water and blood out. Then I positioned her body over the tub with her head down so that she could finish bleeding out. I grabbed a big suitcase from her closet and packed her in it.

Then, I buried the suitcase under a lot of trash in a large dumpster behind a convenience store. That was the end of that muthafucka.

Now I have to find a way to get Sly Davis off my ass or pay him before I get grabbed by the cops again. I don't want to be locked up owing this muthafucka money. I will be a sitting duck in lock up. It would only be a matter of time before some hungry killer bastard executes the hit he would put out on me.

Hmmm, my daddy owes me about 90 thousand in unpaid child support not to mention the compensation I should receive for all the pain and suffering that not having a real daddy has caused me.

I think I'll make this muthafucka have to come up with the money to pay Sly or cause him to die for lack of trying.

Chapter 6

MAMA

*"Our mothers always remain
the strangest, craziest people
we've ever met."*
~ Marguerite Duras

My mama, Melinda Johnson, was a woman of mixed heritage. Her dad was Puerto Rican and mom was Black. Melinda's mother, Renisha Johnson, was beautiful, like a walking work of art. Just like her mother mama has a beautiful face and an hour glass figure.

Many men have dated and thought of marrying her but due to her fits of anger and toxic personality they usually run away very quickly.

Mama is trapped financially because she has no income or means to support herself. She doesn't work because, due to her personality, she cannot hold a job for very long.

Mama has some daddy issues because her real dad (I don't even know who he is because she refuses to speak his name) abandoned her mom just before she was born. And she has low self esteem because her step father used to humiliate her as a young girl as a means of setting her up to be his sex toy when she was a teenager.

Now, at even the least little hint of a personal slight she goes off which makes her socially incapable of interacting properly with people, especially other women, or holding a job.

Mama, therefore, lives off welfare, child support and what she can get from men. She was briefly engaged to a Police Officer, Brad Williams, for whom she thought she had purposely gotten pregnant.

Police Officers have good income and benefits and she wanted to take a good percentage of his pay through child support to support herself for at least 20 years.

So she set out to trick him into getting her pregnant by sucking his dick like Super-Head until she knew he was about to come. Then she would hop on him and ride him raw, pumping like a crazy woman, until he came. She made sure that he came deep inside of her.

Brad thought mama had the best pussy ever. She would fuck him every which way and anywhere: outside in the park, in the car, in back of the movie, she didn't care.

The objective was to keep him excited and thinking about the pussy and not the possibility of having a baby. He was having a good time too until she told him that she was pregnant.

Then he was ready to kill her. That nigga realized immediately that he had literally gotten fucked.

He paid the child support but he never spoke to her again nor has he ever seen me. Brad's mother Maddie kept in touch with mama until I was born. She convinced mama to name me Lashaun.

Maddie tried to kept in touch in order to see her grandson but mama began to avoid her after she recognized that I looked way too Hispanic to be Brad's son.

The truth is mama never got pregnant by Brad. I am actually the son of Hector Pabellón who mama was fuckin the same time as Brad.

Hector is a married man who comes around to fuck my mother on the side, making her his side piece and making me a side piece baby. There are some things that I still have to say about mama so we will get back to this Hector muthafucka later.

The thing that angered me most about mama is the many men that she would allow to sleep in her bed.

When I was about 3 years old I remember waking up after having a nightmare. Just as I sat up in bed a bolt of lightning flashed brightly through my window followed by a loud crack of thunder. Man, was I scared. Noises coming from my mother's room made me even more afraid because it sounded like she might be hurt.

I ran to mama's room but stopped because I caught a glimpse of her through the crack between the wall and the door.

She was naked on the bed with a man who was also naked. He was laying at the edge of the bed with his feet hanging towards the floor. She was standing on the floor facing away from him bouncing on his lap. He was holding her around her waist. I couldn't tell if he was hurting her or not but she was still making those sounds.

Then I saw his dick pop out from between her legs. It looked like it was the same size as my whole body. The sight of that big thing popping out startled me. I remember having to quickly cover my mouth to keep from making a sound.

Mama grabbed it, made a motion real fast up and down with it, and put it back between her legs. Then she started bouncing on his lap again.

I ran back to my room and hid under the covers from the thunder and lightning that continued rage outside of my bedroom window.

The next morning I woke up early and went to see if mama was ok. I looked in her room and there they were sleeping, naked, tangled up in each other's arms.

I was really hungry but I was afraid to wake mama up. So I went to the kitchen, pulled a chair to the counter, climbed up on the counter, and got my cereal out of the cabinet.

I managed to get the gallon jug of milk out of the refrigerator. That was not so bad but getting the milk into the bowl was hard because the jug was heavy. I ended up spilling a lot of it and used almost a whole roll of paper towels trying to clean it up.

When mama came sliding into the kitchen on the back of her house shoes wearing only her night shirt I was already eating. She said "Oh, my baby made his own cereal!" She came over and kissed me. I was happy for a second until I noticed that she smelled like shit. Apparently, they had been having anal sex.

Just then the strange man who had been in mama's bed came into the kitchen. She asked "Are you leaving?" He said "Yeah, gotta go, I'll call you later."

Then he kissed her and at the same time reached both of his hands under her nightshirt and squeezed her butt cheeks. He exposed her butt to me as he slid his hands up from her butt to her waist.

Mama pushed his hands away and said "Stop, the boy." He looked at me and said "Yo mama got a nice ass, don't she little man?" (I wished at that moment that I was big enough to stab him right in his eye with my spoon.)

He laughed and mama laughed. She pushed him toward the door and said "Get outta here wit yo crazy self."

As he walked down the sidewalk laughing mama said "Don't forget to call me." He threw up one hand as if to acknowledge that he heard what she said but didn't turn around to look at her. I never saw him again. I don't think he ever called mama either.

Mama had many men like this come to our house. They would come over to visit one or two times, sleep in her bed, and then never come back. I hated when any of them would say anything to me. I especially hated it when they were trying to be funny and expected me to laugh.

The thing that I hated the most though was every one of them called me "little man" like I didn't have a fuckin name or that they even cared to ask me about.

The only man who ever returned consistently to see my mother was Hector. I didn't know at the time that he was my real father. I have the feeling that he knew I was his son but he rarely ever said one word to me.

Most of the time he just looked at me as he was leaving, having a kind of smirk on his face. Even as a little boy I was offended by the way he looked at me. I thought "Why is this muthafucka always lookin at me with that shit eatn' grin."

Sometimes I wanted to yell "The fuck you lookin at bitch!" But I wasn't old enough to beat the shit out of him yet if he came at me. I vowed to myself that I was going to fuck him up one day.

When I was about 14 mama met and married a man named Leroy Rollings who was from Macon, Georgia. He grew up on a farm down there and was rather a country bama ass nigga that was not mama's usual type.

She usually went for the slick pretty boy type. This cat was different and nice in a down home country way. He was an industrious man who worked hard taking jobs at various factories around the area.

But he was also a gambler and an entrepreneur by nature. He was good at gambling shooting pool and playing cards from which he won often.

I remember one night he came home with a big brown grocery bag full of money and handed it to mama who was in bed at the time. I recall seeing her sitting in the middle of the bed with her legs folded counting the money with her eyes as big as saucers.

He was the man and she was lovin him on the nights he was a big winner. But then I remember the nights he came home after losing big.

She would just go in after him, lashing him with her acid tongue. I said to myself "Oh, so that's how it is. Win and you're the man, but lose and you're a two bit country fuck."

Hey, that was my mama and he loved her. I think she may have seduced him because you could tell he had never been with a woman that looked as good as mama.

I could tell this type of nigga usually went for either hoes or the big girls. He stayed with mama because he liked having sex with her. I would hear him sometimes in mama's bedroom sounding like an old bull banging it out.

She stayed with him because he was a good source of income. But I could tell that she didn't really love him and he knew it too. I think it caused him to drink and he drank a lot.

Sometimes after he passed out mama would go out. I knew where she was going too; to that Hector muthafucka. She was still letting him hit it every now and then. Man, she used to make me mad messing with that muthafucka!

Whenever they had both been drinking mama and Leroy would fight. He would try to beat her ass and she would fight back. They fought all the time; at home and out in the street.

One night he was jacking mama up outside of a bar and this little cat said "Why don't you leave the lady alone." Leroy said "This my wife nigga you betta speed on before you get peed on."

The little cat jumped on him and knocked him down in front of a basement window before he knew what hit him. The joker stomped on him so hard that he crashed through the basement window.

The next time I saw him he was beat the fuck up with almost his whole right are bandaged up. From then mama started carrying a small gun to protect herself when he started going in on her. Sometimes she even had some of her men friends tune him up for her.

They had a crazy and violent relationship but they stayed together for about 11 or 12 years. He was good with getting money and she was good at giving pussy so it worked for them.

Like I said, Leroy was also an entrepreneur or small business man who owned taxi cabs. He always had anywhere from 1 to 5 cabs working at a time that made him good money. He also ran a numbers book that he made good money from. Somebody was always hitting with him and giving him even more on the side.

He even got mama hooked up with her own book. She was making herself some extra change now which gave her kind of an entrepreneur spirit too.

She started hosting card games at the house where people could either buy or bring their own bottle. If they brought a bottle, she would sell them "set-ups" or a glass, ice and chaser.

The games went on for hours and even all night most of the time. So she would sell dinners and sandwiches too. Each time a bet was made, anywhere from a quarter to a dollar had to be put in a cup for the house.

So, off the bets, booze, and food she would do pretty good. Fight night or the TV boxing matches were party time at our house too. Mama would do the same thing and make some pretty good money then too.

Together they kept a lot of money flowing in the house. Mama bought herself a Mustang convertible. She started wearing gowns, furs and dressing up lookin like Dorothy Dandridge and shit.

I have to admit she did know how to make herself look muthafuckin glamorous. On Leroy's part, even when he did put on a suit, his ass still looked country.

Mama used to try to dress him up and make him look sharp. But on him, no matter how expensive, suits still looked like they came from the country store. The only time Leroy looked cool was when he was casual.

He never wore sneakers like Hector's ass. He always wore shoes and pants with these nice knit sweater type shirts with a apple jack style cap.

One day Leroy came home from the factory early and caught Hector in the house. Them muthafuckas was breaking furniture up in there that day. That was a huge fight but Leroy won and stomped the Mexican fuck out of Hector's ass.

Him and mama had a huge fight that day too. I thought he was going to kill her so I had to step in to save her from that ass whuppin. They made up after a few days but it was never the same between them.

Leroy started drinking even more. Going out and staying out for days at a time. He came home one time to get some clothes or something but he had a lady waiting for him in the car. Mama went fuckin ballistic and chased the lady down the street.

They went in the bedroom and argued after that. But then it seemed like they fucked for two days non-stop. Not long after that he was gone and mama, once again, was alone.

****

News of my escape from jail was out and the possible connection to Lola's disappearance so there is a desperate man hunt on.

After the police raided my mother's house, I went to her and begged her to hide me for a few days. I knew they wouldn't be back to search her house again for at least a few days. But she refused and told me that I have to turn myself in.

Then she said, "If you are not man enough to pay the price for your actions, I guess I will have to call and turn you in myself."

I said "Mama, pay the price for my actions? What about you? You haven't been paying the price for your actions? Maybe I wouldn't be fucked up like this if you hadn't been fuckin every man you see from the time I was three.

Maybe if you didn't go out trying to find men every weekend and give the babysitter an opportunity to rape me, I wouldn't have actions to answer for."

Mama was wild eyed furious and said something in response to my plea that totally shocked me. You see, when niggas get mad they will tell you how they really feel.

Mama said "You wasn't getting raped nigga, you was getting fucked and yo dick sucked. Latoya liked having sex with little boys so I didn't have to pay her to watch you. She paid me to fuck you. She liked fuckin you, you liked being fucked but you was too dumb to know not to come in her ass.

I didn't fuck you up nigga, you fucked yo self up. You liked that shit but gonna stand here and tell me it fucked you up. You gonna judge me and tell me I fucked you up? You ain't been fucked up yet until I make this call! Let's see how you like being fucked in lock up."

It was hard to take everything in that she just said so my head was swimming. Then a rage burst on the inside of me and I noticed a clothes iron on the counter.

Before she could finish dialing I grabbed the iron and busted her in the back of the head with it. I hit her but not good enough to knock her out.

She stumbled out of the kitchen and ran into the back of her bedroom. I caught her there and started trying to hit her in the head some more. She was fighting so I was only getting in glancing blows.

She pushed me off balance and tried to run out of the room. I caught her by the door and began bashing her head up against the wall. That finally knocked her out.

I ripped the cord off the iron and tied her hands behind her back. Then I said to myself "This bitch likes muthafuckas to see her naked. The cops and everybody that find yo ass is going to see you naked."

So I tore all of her clothes off and dragged her into another room across the hallway where there was a small sledge hammer in the closet. I used that hammer to bash her face in and beat her to death.

There was a lot of blood and so much of it had splashed on me. I had to change clothes. Being in a daze as I washed mama's blood off my face and hands, I changed clothes, put them in the hamper in my old room and left.

When the police raided her house again after 5 days they found her dead with a bashed in head and half eaten by flies. It didn't take them long to figure out that I had done it because I left my bloody clothes at the scene.

It was stupid but I couldn't think straight because I had just murdered my own mama. In the moment she told me that she pimped me I hated her. But after her murder all I could remember was the times and the things she did to take care of me. I had just gotten too angry. Mama, I am so sorry!

Some homicide detectives finally caught and arrested me. But they didn't have cages in their car to transport a prisoner so they had a patrol officer transport me down to police headquarters.

I don't understand the reason why but this cop was trying to be nice to me. He didn't put the cuffs on too tight and he let the window down so I could get some air when I asked him to.

Then, he parked the car and went inside headquarters but left me in the car with my window still down. The window had bars across it but I still saw an opportunity to escape.

So I worked my cuffs from the back to the front. Pumped out globs of spit to lubricate one side and slipped the cuff off. It hurt like hell but I forced my arm through the flimsy bars to open the door from the outside and I was gone.

They hadn't taken my money yet and I was close to the bus station. I hit Rochester and then paid for a ride to Syracuse. Nobody would ever think to look for me there. Once again I am free but still on the run.

Chapter 7

GESELLE

"There is nothing nobler or more admirable than when two people who see eye to eye keep house as man and wife, confounding their enemies and delighting their friends."
~ **Homer**

Geselle Montalvo is an average looking 36 year old Puerto Rican woman with a thick accent. Her teeth are a little bucked in the front but she has a cute face, long black hair, and a shy smile.

There is nothing physically special about Geselle except she is tall, 5'8", 165 lbs with small breasts, skinny legs and wide hips for a woman that doesn't have any children.

****

I was on the streets of Syracuse and on the run so I need a place to lay low and a way to make some dough. I can't call Sheila, Laneesha or anybody connected to me because it might make it easy for the cops to find me. I ducked into a Rite Aid Drug Store to see if they have a phone book so I could try to find a cheap place to stay.

As I was flipping through the phone book I looked down the counter to my right and I saw a Puerto

Rican woman looking at me. When I looked at her she smiled shyly and turned her head. I thought to myself "Aw shucks, this may be the opportunity I need."

I walked over to her and said "Hey mami, you sure are pretty can I ask your name." She said "Geselle" and stuck out her hand to shake mine. I said "Listen, I was about to grab lunch at Arby's across the street. Would you mind having a sandwich with me?"

She hesitated so I said "It's only lunch. It's lunch time, you gotta eat lunch right?" She smiled and said "Ok, it's only lunch."

We were crossing the street at the corner when a car pulled up to the light fast getting kind of close to Geselle before stopping. I grabbed her by the waist and pulled her to the other side of me to protect her and she liked that.

We sat in Arby's two hours talking, laughing, and having fun. So I looked at my watch and said "Boy, I've been having so much fun I forgot why I went into Rite Aid. I told her that I came to Syracuse for the day with some friends, had gotten separated from them and needed to get back to Buffalo.

I said "But I've had so much fun with you it seems like losing my friends was a touch of fate orchestrated by GOD so that I could meet you." Then I moved closer to her and said "I really don't want to leave without getting to know you better. Do you think we could spend some more time together... alone?"

She looked in my eyes as if she was half ass hypnotized and said "We could hang out at my place and I can make dinner." Inside of myself I said "Yeah muthafucka!" Outside of myself I said "That would be beautiful."

We walked back across the street to where her car was parked in the drug store parking lot and I began to sense that this chick may be more than she appeared to be.

She was pushing a Lexus IS 250. That car is understated in appearance, just like Geselle, but it is a high performance luxury vehicle. This is the kind of car people who got dough drive that is trying to keep it on the low. So now, I'm starting to look at her differently and thinking I'd better keep my eyes open.

Geselle has a nice house in a working-class neighborhood. It is very clean outside with a manicured lawn. Inside, this chick's house is laid out. The kitchen appliances were top of the line and there was a built in wine bottle refrigerator or cooler. She had cherry wood floors in the dining room that were gleaming. The living room was totally plushed out; thick carpet, huge soft furniture, with the biggest flat screen TV that I've ever seen.

She took my jacket, handed me the remote and a glass of wine and said "Here, try this. If you want to take a shower, the bathroom is upstairs." I had only seen a bathroom like hers in magazines or the movies. It had a double sink vanity and a huge Jacuzzi tub next to a 3 head shower.

As I was taking a shower she came in and laid out a man's set of silk pajamas and a brand new package of boxer brief underwear. I was thinking to myself "This is fuckin amazing!"

As I was getting out of the shower I could tell that she was already cooking and boy did it smell good. Within a half hour she had whipped up this, like, buffet of Puerto Rican dishes that looked and tasted so good it is indescribable: Carne Guisada (Stewed Beef), Arroz con Gandules (Rice with Pigeon Peas), Pernil (Roast Pork) and pollo agridulce (sweet and sour chicken).

I forgot what she called it but it was actually cornbread that had cheese, corn and broccoli in it. I was having such a good time eating, joking, and drinking wine that I forgot that I was supposed to be on alert.

After eating Geselle took me upstairs to her bedroom and had me sit in an armchair while she sat on the side of the bed. Then she said "Now, tell me. Why did you actually come on to me today?"

I started saying "Well, because you…" Her tone changed and she said "No, nigga, the truth!" Then she slid a sliver handgun from under the pillow. I said "Whoa, ok, here's the truth."

I told her that I was wanted for murder but I was innocent. I also told her how I had been slinging weed, rock, heroine and doing robberies. I spilled everything about how I had been locked up and how I had killed muthafuckas but I was innocent of the one they wanted me for. I told her that it was this nigga I owed 90k who was taking people that I love away and making it look like I did it.

She said "When I first saw you today I could sense you had baller skills. You are a young nigga but have done a lot of living for your age. I could see that. You came on to me with that school boy shit so I decided to play the school girl just to check you out. Now that I know you are desperate, on the run, and you got baller skills, you may just be the one I've been looking for son! She popped the clip out of the gun, walked over and put it in the dresser.

She took off her shirt exposing some nice but small titties and said "So let's see how you good are with the pussy."

I needed some pussy right then so I started digging that back out. I knew that I was auditioning for something, although I didn't know what, so I was gonna give her a grand performance. I turned her ass every way but loose. It turned out she was a squirter so she was comin all over the place.

When I was hittin it doggie style the sight of her asshole reminded me of Jasmine's and it looked like she might have been getting hit in there too. So as I was plugging her from the back I started massaging her asshole with my thumb.

Then I took my dick and put it on there and said "May I enter ma'am?" She said "Yes, sir, you may!" I started rockin that ass like I was hittin Jasmine: hard, fast and deep making my dick disappear between her butt cheeks. Geselle started screaming and comin just like Jasmine did.

When I came in her ass the orgasm was intense so I fell down on the bed. She said "Oh, nigga, I gotta suck yo dick, I gotta suck yo dick." She almost sprinted to the bathroom, got a wash cloth, and washed it off. Then she began to make love to my dick with her mouth just like Jasmine. I had to open my eyes a few times and look at Geselle just to make sure that it wasn't Jasmine.

When she sensed that I was about to come or maybe that she was about to come, she hopped on my dick and started bouncing her hips so fast that when I came she made me scream. Just as I started to come, she screamed and came too, splashing my stomach pretty good with her milky white love lotion.

Then she plopped down on my chest and said "Sorry, I got you all wet." I put my arms around her and said "That's ok baby." And we fell asleep just like that.

The next morning I woke up and hit the shower. She came in after me and I busted that ass again in there. Geselle didn't really look like much compared to other women I've been with but damn that pussy was good. She made me stand with both my hands touching the walls of the shower, almost like a crucifix, so that she could wash me.

She washed my body gently. Then got on her knees and washed my dick and balls so sensually, stroking my joint with soap all over her hand, she almost made me come again.

She let the water wash off the soap and then sucked, licked and kissed on the head. Then she stood up and as if talking to my dick said "That's enough for you mister." When she turned around, I pushed her head down and started driving my dick as hard, fast and deep between her butt cheeks as I could.

Just as she let out a mad scream, I came so forcefully my whole body was shaking. I was trying to say "Damn this pussy is good." But the sounds coming out of my mouth were more like something you would hear a retarded Pre-K school kid say.

I got out of the shower and was so weak from the intense orgasm that I could barely dry myself off. I landed face up on the bed. Geselle came out and dove on top of me. And we immediately fell asleep again in a tangled half wet naked mesh of legs and arms, all fucked out.

It was after 2 in the afternoon when we finally woke up. Geselle jumped up, went downstairs, and started cooking. This girl was like a fuckin magician in the kitchen. She was whipping up these great meals fast like waiving a wand.

When I came in the kitchen she had that knife moving in rapid fashion chopping up stuff and throwing it in the pan to sauté in olive oil: garlic, pork roast, ham, peppers, onions, olives, tomatoes, and these little sausages called chorizo. Man, she had the kitchen smelling so good.

She was making Asopao which is a stew or soup like gumbo. To go with it she made these big ass homemade biscuits and poured a Brunello di Montalcino red wine. This girl was spoiling me with all this good food, good wine, and premium pussy.

While we are eating Geselle revealed who she really was and what she wanted. "My last man was moving major cocaine weight in Syracuse and Onondaga County. The feds raided him at one of our stash houses.

He saw them gearing up to come in the front so he grabbed his getaway bag, you know, a bag with a lot of cash passports and all of that stuff you need to survive on the run. (I said to myself "Damn I wish I had thought of that.") Anyway, he grabbed a gun and tried to dash out the back not knowing they were in the back too. When they saw the gun they just started firing and blew him away.

That was almost 2 years ago but here's the thing. There was another stash of 5 uncut kilos the feds didn't get. That is almost a half million dollars just sitting there that I don't know how to move. I couldn't trust anyone that he knew to know that I have it so I couldn't go to them. My proposition is for you to move it for 50% of the profits."

I took another sip of wine and thought about what she said trying to calculate the logistics and risk. Then I said to her "There is a lot I don't know about this area. I've never been here before so this might as well be a foreign country to me. I don't know who the players are, their territories, the market or the demand to be able to estimate how fast a kilo will move."

She smiled recognizing that I knew the distribution "business" of drug marketing and said "I can put you down on all of that and take care of the muscle out of my end."

I said, "Cool but when it comes to the muscle you can select them but have to qualify them muthafuckas. There are a lot of niggas out here who will shoot a muthafucka when they got the upper hand but will fold up like a bitch when they gettin shot at.

You see, a sheep can act like a wolf but he can never be a wolf because a sheep won't eat meat. When it comes down to it I need niggas who have a natural instinct to gobble a muthafucka up! So show me at least 10 niggas. I will pick 5 and put 2 on point watching my back and 3 in reserve just in case we have to roll heavy on some muthafuckas at any time."

"But listen, Geselle, I said, we have to pay them really good to keep these niggas committed. Even the cats in reserve have to be paid everyday even though they are not working every day. You understand?"

"Yeah Mr. Man, I got cha" she said smiling. "Cool, I said, let's go to work."

****

Three months go by and everything is going well. I've gotten back into pushing my MJ as a side hustle and we are reuppin with heroine and coke. Everybody on the team is happy because they are making money. I've already started working my normal hours again: 7AM-6PM so I can be home with Geselle at night.

I came home one evening and she was on the couch but got up quickly and headed toward the kitchen as I came in the door. She said "I cooked, baby, you hungry?" Before she got up though I noticed her eyes looked like she'd been crying.

As she was standing at the stove I went up behind her and grabbed her around the waist and asked "Why have you been crying?" She turned around and said "Because I'm pregnant." I said "What, wow, aren't you happy?"

She said "No I'm confused because I don't know if I want to keep it." "Oh" I said, backing up and sitting down on a stool. "I would be happy to have a baby with you but it's your body and your decision. I'm with you no matter what." She started crying again, came over and grabbed my face with both of her hands and said "That is exactly what I needed to hear" then kissed me.

When our baby girl, Naomi Lashanda Johnson, was born business was going very well. We were rolling in dough stacking back more than we can spend.

I was sitting in the nursery one morning feeding my baby and suddenly I recalled what Sheila's father said to me. I love this baby so much and now I'm beginning to fear that all of my sins may be visited upon her. I started crying because of all the robberies and murders I had done; especially killing mama.

So I put Naomi in her crib, went into the bedroom, and began weeping uncontrollably. For the first day ever in my life I prayed and asked GOD to forgive me and to not allow my sins to be visited upon my innocent baby. At that moment, just like Sheila's dad Frank, I knew that I had to change.

Two days later as I was on my way to work I saw a billboard advertising a women's conference the following Saturday at the OnCenter. One of the featured speakers is my first baby's mama Sheila Jemison. I was shocked because I had just been thinking about her and her father.

I checked for the event details online and looked for Sheila in particular. Her biography stated that she was now an evangelist who spoke to women about relationships from the Bible perspective. All of a sudden I started seeing these billboards everywhere. I went into a store and there were flyers on the counter advertising it. I grabbed one and put it in my pocket.

When I got home I put everything in my pockets on the dresser and hit the shower. Geselle was in the room looking at the flyer when I came out of the shower and asked "What is this?" I said "It's just a flyer that caught my eye."

She said "Isn't your other baby's mama named Sheila Jemison?" I said "Yes, that is her." "Do you plan to see her?" she asked. "No, I cannot afford to let anyone from there know that I'm here. Everything is going so good, I cannot take a chance and blow it now" I said. "Good, she said, but just know that if you go anywhere near that bitch I will cut her" and walked out of the room.

The day of the conference came and something was drawing me to it. I went to work at 7AM as usual but it was all I could think about. The conference started at 10AM so around 11 I had one of the cats post up for me and went to the OnCenter to see what was drawing me. My intention was to just stand in the crowd to watch and listen to see what happens.

The place was packed with women; more women than I had ever seen in one place in my life. Several women spoke, one right after another, and had the ladies in the crowd rocking, laughing, cheering, and high-fiving each other. They were also saying things that got me to thinking about the direction of my life.

One lady said: "People have multiple troubles through their life because they cannot reconcile the image of who they want people to think they are with who they really are. A house divided against its self cannot stand so they fall repeatedly."

Then she said "It was hard for me to lose weight at one time because I didn't see myself as a fat girl. That is, until one day I walked past the mirror and got scared because I thought somebody had broken in the house. Once I saw myself as I really was then it was easier for me to change!"

Another lady said: "Walk away from a man who is less interested in learning what's inside the space above your face than he is in entering that space below your waist."

That one really hit me because all I am ever really interested in is the pussy. I don't really care about what a girl thinks or feels. I am only interested in them if they look good and I will only stay with them as long as the pussy is good. I was really starting to see that it was time for me to change.

When Sheila came to the stage a number of things she said struck my heart and really made me begin to see me.

After reading John 12:24, "Except a corn of wheat fall into the ground and dies, it will live alone: but if it dies, it will bring forth much fruit, she said: "Many marriages fail and many men end up being alone because they refuse to die to being that single little boy they are used to being.

Many adult males never become men because they refuse to die to being boys. They still like to hang out with the boys because they are like a seed in a bag in the barn hanging out with the other seeds.

One corn seed was designed by GOD to produce many ears of corn or many other corn seeds. But not many men produce today anything other than unwanted babies because they refuse to die to their boy-like nature and be planted in the right place, at the right time, and with the right WOMAN (the crowd cheered in agreement), to reach their full potential."

Near the end of her speech she said "Finally, ladies, in order to have a good marriage you have to have a good man who, first, knows and understands GOD's two greatest commandments: Love GOD and Love your neighbor as you love yourself.

Second, he has to know how to love his wife as he loves himself." Then she said "I have never met a man that could use, abuse or physically harm a woman who loved himself. In order to love somebody as you love yourself, you have to first love yourself.

Love, empathy and compassion for yourself give you the capacity to extend those to others. If a man loves Jesus, loves others and loves you, you can have joy and live in peace with that man because JOY is just an acronym that means: Jesus, Others and You!"

Sheila walked off the stage with the crowd cheering and it touched me. They really seemed to love her. Well, I really shouldn't be surprised because all the girls in high school loved her too.

She was always smart, poised and pretty as a girl. But now as a woman she is exuding beauty elegance and intelligence. I was impressed and feeling happy for her.

I sat in that seat for a while thinking what I had heard and what I want to do with my life. Then looked at my watch "Shit it's 2PM! I stayed here way longer that I planned. I had better get my ass back to the post.

Geselle had gone shopping with Naomi that morning and the whole time the baby just kept saying "da-da, da-da, da-da". Geselle said to her "You must want to see your daddy." So before going home Geselle brought her by the post so she could see me.

She learned that I wasn't there and became angry because she figured that I must have gone to the convention to see Sheila. The more she thought about it the more she became crazy angry. So she decided to drive up to the OnCenter to confront me.

As I dashed out the front door Sheila came out of a service exit and we bumped right into each other. "Lashaun!" she said in an excited scream and hugged me. "Oh my GOD, I was afraid you might be dead or something" and hugged me again. I said "Yeah, you know I got into some trouble, as usual, and had to go on the run."

How is Raven?" I asked. "She is fine, growing real fast, and she is so pretty and funny. I hope you get everything taken care of and finally get free so that you can get to know her and she can get to know her real daddy." I said "Yeah, I know that I have to... No, I have already decided that it is time for me to change."

I said "Sheila, I have to apologize to you because you were good to me, you loved me, and I just went around cheating on you. I was trying not to cheat but for some reason I couldn't stop." "Don't worry about that son, she said playfully, we were just kids and you didn't know how to love yet. When you love someone you don't concentrate on not cheating, you concentrate on loving. When you really love someone, you won't have to TRY not to cheat."

Then she said "The foundation of sin is selfishness. The only reason I ended up pregnant with Raven is not because I cared so much about you it was because I didn't want to lose you to those other girls. It wasn't about winning you. I was about beating them.

I really liked you Lashaun but I didn't really love you as much as I loved myself. My wanting to be with you was a simple act of selfishness. But everything for me turned out for the good: you were a lessin' and my baby is a blessin'."

She hugged me and kissed me on the cheek and said "It was good seeing you but I've got to go; gotta catch a plane to NY City." I asked her "Please don't tell anybody you saw me." She said "As usual, I got you boo" as she quickly walked away heading for her car.

I stood and watched her for a minute then began heading for my car. I turned to catch another glimpse of her and I saw Geselle's car pull up next to her fast and stop. Apparently, this crazy chick must have seen me talking to Sheila.

"Oh shit!" I said as I ran toward them yelling Geselle, Geselle!" Before I could reach them she jumped out of the car and struck Sheila in the face twice with a box cutter. When Sheila went down she cut a plug of her hair out from the top of her head, threw it at her and said "You mess with my man you mess with my money, bitch!"

I grabbed Geselle from behind being sure to control both of her arms, swung her around, and pinned her up against her car. "You gotta get outta here before the cops come!" I yelled to her. She said "Let me go, nigga, this shit is on you. I told you not to go near this bitch or I was going to cut her."

I said "Please, just get in the car and go before the cops come! Go, Go!" When I let her go she jumped in the car and said "Usted me hizo tener que coger a esta perra, lo que está en usted!; You made me have to fuck this bitch up. This is on you!" as she sped off.

I looked down at Sheila and she was really bleeding. I took off my shirt and ripped up my t-shirt so she could have something to press against the cuts to slow down the bleeding and called for an ambulance. Now, a crowd was starting to form around us asking what happened.

I asked this lady if she would help Sheila hold the make-shift bandage against her face so I could get a first aid kit from my car. She said "Yes, go I'll help her." I went to the car and took off. I could not afford to be there if the cops showed up and started asking questions. I hated to leave Sheila there like that but I had to.

I was so mad at Geselle I didn't know what to do. I had it in my mind to fuck her up to teach her a lesson. That shit was not smart. Now we are going to have police attention that we do not need.

I burst into the house through the kitchen door and yelled "Geselle!" She came out of the pantry, racked the slide on her .25, held it up to my face and said "What muthafucka!"

I leaned my head away from the barrel of the gun and said "Whoa, bitch, you pullin a gun on me? This shit is un muthafuckin acceptable! Put that fuckin gun down!" She said "No, while trying to track my head movement with the barrel, you brought this shit on. I told you not to go see that bitch but you went anyway. This shit is on you!"

I told her "I didn't go there to see her. I just happened to bump into her. I went there for our baby!" "What the fuck you mean our baby?" she said. I said "Wait, let me sit down" while backing up on the stool.

I told her the whole story about Frank kidnapping me, what he had said, and what happened in the baby's room a few days ago. Then I told her that I went there to hear something about how to be a better man in general and a better father to my baby. And that I actually did learn some shit that made me know I need to grow the fuck up.

I said "The last thing I wanted to do was see Sheila. Like I told you before, I cannot afford to have anybody from there know that I'm here but that's all fucked up now."

She put down the gun and said "I'm so sorry baby, what are we going to do?" I said "I don't know what you are going to do. Hopefully, nobody saw you or knows who you are but as for me I cannot sit here and wait to see if the cops show up. I have to go back on the run." She cried and said "I'm so sorry. I don't want you to go" but she knew that I had to.

Luckily, thanks to Geselle's connections, I already had a getaway bag with fake ID and driver license, social security card, passport, credit card, clothes, toiletries, and $150,000 cash ready.

She asked "Where will you go?" I told her "It is safer if you don't know. This way if the cops get up on you it will be harder for them to trace me. I'm going to take two burners with me.

If you see anything about me in the newspaper or on TV, use one of the other burners and text the word "UP" to one of these phones so I will know that they are up on me. I will destroy that phone after I receive the text.

117

Do not make any calls because they can find my location from the tower the phone is pinging off. After a month if you have not been contacted or heard anything about me text the word "CLEAN" to the other phone and I will be getting in touch with you within a week or so from that day.

In the meantime, keep them niggas posted up. Tell them I had to go out of town on business and that I will be back in a few weeks." We kissed and I jetted.

Chapter 8

HECTOR

"Woe to the man who offends a small child!"
~ Fyodor Dostoyevsky

Hector Aviles-Pabellón, Lashaun's biological father, is a handsome 43 year old Puerto Rican man who, like his son, was a rebellious youth throughout his teens and early 20's. He grew tired of going to jail and got a job in Sheehan Hospital as a janitor when he was 24 and has been working there ever since.

Hector is married with 5 children from his wife of 18 years Maria Santiago-Pabellón. But he has another 7 kids with 6 other women who were all born while married to Maria. Hector does know about these children and still frequently sleeps with some of their mothers. Yet, he provides no financial, emotional or paternal support to any of them. He only takes care of the 5 kids from his wife.

Hector was able to get away with this because Maria does not care that he cheats. She established a line he can't cross or a code of conduct he must maintain that as long as she remains #1, he tells the women that he is married, and he doesn't throw any of his bitches up in her face he can do what he wants.

Maria says "These bitches know that he is a married man but they throw their pussy at him anyway. My man likes pussy like a dog likes steak. Love of pussy is in his nature, a part of his character, and I cannot change that. You throw a steak at a dog and he is going to eat it. He is not going to say my owner doesn't want me to eat table food. He is going to wolf down that steak fast as he can, lick his lips, and act just like he never had nothing!

At the end of the day Hector comes home to me. I get all of his money and those bitches don't get shit but a hard dick in their mouth or ass. I'm tired of having babies. If these bitches want to keep giving him pussy and having his babies that is fine with me. In fact, they are actually helping me keep his ass off me."

****

One day me and mama were shopping in the Galleria Mall and we saw Hector with his wife. Mama kind of stared at them and when Hector saw her looking at him he smiled at her. Maria noticed mama looking at them like she knew Hector and saw the little smile on Hector's face so she started going off on him. She was throwing shit at him and cussin his ass out in Spanish: "Te dije que to guarde estas perras de mi cara; I told you to keep these bitches out of my face!"

I was happy to see somebody standing up to that muthafucka and letting him have it. Next she looked at mama and yelled at her too: "¿Qué diablos estás

120

mirando perra; what the fuck is you looking at bitch!" She acted like she wanted to come towards mama.

Hector grabbed her around the waist, pulled her to him, and started walking her away as he whispered "Ella no significa mada para ser bebé; she means nothing to be baby." "Yo no quiero ver na ninguno de sus putas; I don't want to see none of your whores" Maria warned him. "Sé bebé Yo sé; I know baby, I know" I could hear Hector say as they walked away.

About a week or so before this incident Hector asked me out of the clear blue if I wanted him to bring me anything the next time he came over. Since he rarely said anything to me the question caught me off guard. So, I said "Let me think". Then I remembered something I thought of having a little while back.

Mama liked to go to Spot Coffee on Elmwood which is in a kind of ritzy part of town where rich people live. As we were driving down this side street over there I saw a big stone building that said "Nardin High School" on top.

Then I saw two white boys, who had to be rich, waiting for a girl and calling for her to hurry up as she walking down the steps. They had on matching rain jackets, navy blue on the outside and yellow on the inside, along with matching boots. They were navy blue rubber boots with beige across the area of the laces. I thought they looked so cool. First, I thought to myself "Somebody gotta explain to me why I ain't got shit. Then I said "I'm gonna be rich and then I'm gonna dress like that one day."

121

I described the rain jacket and boots to Hector. Then he bent down so that we were face to face and he said "Ok, they're yours little man." I wanted to round house kick him right in the teeth when he said "little man" but I didn't want to mess things up.

I couldn't wait until Hector came over again. I asked mama several times when he was coming back. She kept saying that she didn't know then she yelled at me one day and told me to stop asking.

When Hector finally did come over he was empty handed. I asked him if he had forgotten what he promised and he said "Get away from me little muthafucka!" He grabbed mama by the back of her neck, pushed her in the bedroom, and slammed the door.

I heard sounds like they are fighting at first about the incident at the mall. After a little while I heard the bed creaking. I went into my room and closed the door so I wouldn't have to listen to that shit. That is when I first started making actual plans in my head about what I was going to do to this muthafucka when I got old enough.

****

After leaving Syracuse I figured the best place to hide was in plain sight. If the cops were hunting for me in Syracuse they would not think to look for me in Buffalo. Besides mama, as far as they would know, I had no more connections to Buffalo.

I checked into a nice suite at the Hyatt Regency Hotel downtown within walking distance from some hot night clubs, restaurants and the theater district. I stayed away from any places in the inner city where there may be shooting or the cops might appear suddenly. Unless they were middle to upper class associating with Black people was a no go.

When low class niggas party they think they have to wild out which sometimes causes trouble and attracts cops. So I hung out downtown partying with and picking up white chicks and Asian girls. I missed Naomi and Geselle but I was having a good time.

No matter how good you lay low or limit the places where you go you will always unexpectedly run into somebody you know. I had a taste for some baby-back bar-b-q ribs and TGI Friday's had the best in that area. It was down the street from the hotel so as I walked to the restaurant I noticed a lot of Black people milling around on Main Street.

I looked up at the marquis on Shea's Performing Arts Center and Chris Tucker was performing. I guess a lot of people decided to eat at Friday's before going to the show. I said to myself "I'm glad I ordered my food to go so I can get it and jet back to my hideout."

As soon as I grabbed my food and turned around there was Laneesha. We were standing just about face to face. She screamed and yelled "My nigga!"

She was with three other people, a cat and two girls, who I had never seen before. I quickly moved past them so they couldn't get a good look at my face. I started saying "Hey girl..." looking for a way to play the situation off and she said "Nope come with me." I said "Where..." but she cut me off and said "Shut up and come with me".

At the same time she was giving one of the girls she was with the "I'll call you" sign with her fingers and mouthing it to her also. She led me outside and said "Where is your car?" I told her I walked down here. I'm staying down the street at the Hyatt hotel." She said "Let's go."

When we got up to the room she grabbed my bag and said "This shit was smellin good in the elevator and I'm hungry as hell." She took a knife, cut off a couple of bones, kicked off her shoes, hopped on the bed bouncing and said "Ok, nigga, tell me the story."

I said "What story?" First she gave me that you know what the fuck I'm talkin about look then she said "You know that escape from jail, runnin away, and killin yo mama shit story nigga! Where have you been and what you been doin?" I said "It's a long story."

She said "Well gimme a piece of that bread and some more meat and tell me the story." I said "You are so funny, I missed you." She said "Yeah, I missed you and I want to kiss you but tell me the story first nigga!"

We ate as I told her the whole damn story from Lola to mama, from escape from jail to life with

Geselle. She said "Wow, you have really been through some shit man. This sounds like some shit them Hollywood muthafuckas might make into a movie."

She got up off the bed, walked over to the vanity, and washed her mouth with Listerine. As she walked I noticed her little booty looked kind of fat in that dress and now I was getting horny.

I said "How about that kiss now." She said "Stand up. I know what I want to kiss." She pulled down my pants and started sucking my dick and when it got real hard she said "Oooo nigga I almost forgot what you workin with." Then she stood up, stepped out of her panties, backed me up against the wall, and hopped up to get her monkey fuck on.

When I slipped my dick between the lips of that warm wet pussy it felt so good. I kissed her passionately and said "Damn I missed you." She screamed and came right then even before I had a chance to get in one stroke.

I had to keep kissing her to muffle the loud sound coming out of her mouth as she started doing her monkey hump. Only this time she was doing it slower and plunging my dick deeper into her pussy than ever before.

We kept kissing, the pussy was feeling amazing, and she started crying. I had never seen this tough as nails, shoot a muthafucka in the head without blinking, crazy chick cry before.

I realized then that I wasn't just fuckin her like all the other times. This lady that I worked for in a restaurant, who was about as old as my mama, taught me how to really make love to a woman instead of just fucking her. I was actually making love to Laneesha for the first time.

I don't think she ever had a man make love to her. Her step daddy and every other man simply fucked her but nobody cared enough to make love to her. "Shit, I thought to myself, am I starting to care about muthafuckas?" I don't know about other muthafuckas but I do know that I care about Laneesha.

She is a girl but she is just as good of a road dog as any dude. I took her over to the bed and we continued to make love until we had our fill and both fell asleep.

The next morning Laneesha had something to do so she got up early and left but we made plans to hook up later. I went downstairs to use the fitness center and got grabbed by Sly's right hand man Rock in the lobby.

He showed me the handle of his gun and said "I heard you were back in town son. Sly wants to talk to you. If you make a scene or try to run I will plug your ass right here and you will be done."

Whoever that nigga Laneesha was with must have figured out, based on how she reacted when seeing me, that I must be the one that she knew who Sly was looking for. If a nigga want to find you all they have to do is keep tabs on your friends. Hanging far back, he followed us to see where we were going. He called one of Sly's people and told him where I was.

Rock was a deadly one-eyed scar face muthafucka. Somebody had knifed him in the face leaving a scar across his left eye from the middle of his forehead down to his cheek. He lost his eye due to the injury and replaced it with a glass eye.

Anybody can tell it's not a real eye which makes him look even more scary. I don't think it's a real glass eye either. It looks like that muthafucka just stuck one of those big cat-eye marbles in his fuckin head.

Although he is a cold blooded killer even if you didn't know that his whole appearance and demeanor says he is somebody that you don't want to fuck with.

When we came out of the hotel Rock had two of his boys waiting outside. Laneesha was still outside too in her car on the phone calling up to my room. She had changed her plans and wanted me to come with her to Delaware Park on a 5 mile run. She saw them put me in the car and followed us looking for an opportunity to either help or rescue me.

They took me over to Brewster Street in a rundown area of town where most of the houses were torn down. There was only about 4 or 5 houses left on the whole street. In the basement of one of them Sly had a torture chamber set up to deal with people who do not fulfill his will.

I knew that I had to come up with a good story to keep Sly from killing me. I also knew he hated Hispanic men with a passion. He had a drug deal go bad with some Columbians from the Cali Cartel where he got shot in the knee, which gave him a permanent limp, and which is when Rock lost his eye.

So he did not care if you were Puerto Rican, Mexican, Cuban or whatever. If you were a Hispanic male and you crossed him, he was going to find a way to make you pay. Torture was his favorite pleasure for dealing with people who crossed him. So I decided to give this muthafucka that muthafuckin Hector.

Rock and his boys took me in the basement and cuffed both my arms and legs to a chair that was bolted into the cement floor next to a huge drain. I looked at the drain and thought to myself that it must make it easy for them to get rid of the blood.

Just then I heard Sly's big, elderly pimp, Jay Anthony Brown, lookin ass limping down the stairs.

He walked over to me and said "I finally got yo ass." I said "Sly, you have every right to kill me and I'm ready to die but please just listen to me first." He took a step back and said "Ok muthafucka say what you gotta say but it better be somethin good."

I said "First of all I have your money. One of the reasons I came back was to pay you. I have $103,000 in cash in a bag under the bed in my hotel room. The key card is in my pocket and you can send one of your boys to get it.

128

Rock reached in my pocket, grabbed the card and gave it to one of the cats. He took off the get the bag.

As we waited for the cat to get back Sly pulled a chair up and sat down in front of me. He said "Lashaun I always liked yo ass. You seemed like a smart kid with hustler's chops that wasn't afraid to use a gun. I gave you that deal as a test to see how good you could manage that much product.

My hope was that you would do good and instead of being an independent dealer I could have you representing me in the contract negotiations of my international shipments. But you fucked up and now I have to deal with this shit."

Just then the cat returned with my bag and handed it to Rock. Rock slammed it on the table while staring at me, ripped it open, and after examining it said to Sly "It's all here boss, maybe even a little more."

He was still staring at me but this time with a little smile. Sly said "Look at them bills and make sure they real so we don't get fucked with no counterfeit and make this shit even worse." Rock inspected several stacks randomly pulling a bill out of each one to check them thoroughly and said "It's all good boss."

Sly patted me on the knee and said "I'm proud that you came through with the money son but as you know it is not just about the money it is also about the principle. When word gets out on the street that a man ran off with your $100k and he didn't have to pay, that makes it bad for business. Then, everybody else gets the idea that they can rob you too.

So, even though you made good on the money somebody still has to pay in blood. This way any other would be robbers will know the risk of losing their life may not be as great as the monetary reward."

I told him "The man you really want is Hector Pabellón. If it was not for him double crossing me and stealing your original money, I would have paid you and we would not have had this problem." He said "Hector who?" with his interest peaking at just the sound of a Spanish name.

"Hector Pabellón, I repeated, he is my biological father. Sly laughed and said "I never would have guessed a nigga named Lashaun Johnson was half a spic!"

I knew that Sly was getting angry so I had to get my story out quick. I figured he had to have heard about Lola's and mama's murders being connected to me. I said "If it wasn't for Hector crossing me I wouldn't have had to kill mama and Lola." Now he was getting interested and said "So tell me what happened."

"Lola found my product stash in her basement, I began, and didn't know what to do so she called my mother. I didn't want to keep your cash with the stash so I hid the money at my mother's house.

My mother, with her conniving ass, figured that if I had drugs I had to have money. If I had money, it had to be in the house and it would be hidden in my room. She tossed my room and found it. Hector had spent the night with her so when she found the money and saw her holding it he took it from her.

Mama told me that to make sure I was out of the way this Hector muthafucka called Lola. He told her that she should call the FBI and snitch on me so that she wouldn't get caught up in my shit, go to jail and have her children taken. That is exactly what this bitch did and that is why I murdered her ass.

I also had to take my mama out for siding with Hector over me and scheming to send me to the penitentiary. The only thing is I got lucky and escaped from police custody. I couldn't hang around too long. So I had to jet out before they caught up to me and I didn't get a chance to get to Hector, kill his ass, and get your money!"

Sly looked over at Rock with sort of a blank stare then smiled and yelled "Can I pic'em? Is this a bad muthafucka or what?"

They all started laughing. One of the cats said to Rock "That little nigga bad as you." "Nah, that nigga worse than me. He quick to put a hoe down that's low down. And his mama too, wooo!" Rock said laughing as he dapped the cat up.

Sly signaled to one of the cats to uncuff me and said "Where can we find this Hector muthafucka?" I told Sly that he should be at work and he sent Rock's boys to scoop him up.

When they brought Hector in he was hog tied and gagged with his head bagged. They cuffed him to the chair and removed the bag.

When he saw me Hector said "What, is this about you? You killed your mother now you are going to kill your father too?" I said "Oh, now I'm your son, bitch? That's never how you treated me. I should have killed you when I was three muthafucka! But I'm not going to kill you, Sly is going to deal with you." "Why, Hector said, who the fuck is Sly?"

Sly slapped him hard across the face with his walking stick that opened a gash in his cheek and said "You are about to find out muthafucka!"

Hector screamed and started crying immediately. I had never seen a man bitch up that fast. As tough as he acted while terrorizing my mother, I expected him to be strong and defiant but he folded up like luggage; begging and pleading.

I got so sick hearing him beg that I punched him in the mouth twice hard enough to knock some teeth out and said "Shut the fuck up and man up muthafucka! All the times you acted tough and now you folding up like a pussy. Shut the fuck up!"

Hector said "What did I do?" Sly said "That is what we are here to find out. Lashaun said that you stole his money from his mother which was my money is that true?"

"No that is not true, Hector said, I never stole no money from his mama. She never had no money. The

132

only thing that bitch had worth anything was that pussy." He said that with a little chuckle as he spit out some blood. I said "Ok, now you manning up muthafucka."

Then I said to Sly "The thing that this nigga does best is lie. We can question him all day and all he is going to do is lie. Let me put some pressure on this muthafucka to untwist his tongue."

Sly said "Go ahead and give it a try." I asked Rock's boys "Do ya'll have a toe spreader (a contraption that isolates the toes or spreads them so you can work on each toe one by one)?"

They looked at each other then looked at me and said "Yeah!" at the same time. I said "Let's get it on him." They looked at Sly, he nodded. The one cat laid the spreader down and the other one took off Hector's sneaker and sock.

When the guy took off Hector's sock the funk filled the room and almost at the same time everybody said "Ohhhhhhhooooo!" The cat who took off the sock jumped up and said "Do you ever wash yo feet muthafucka? That smells like some exorcist shit!"

Hector had a bad case of athlete's foot from wearing sneakers all the time with dried cracked skin and green toe nails. When they put the spreader on and clamped it to the floor Hector screamed again. They handed me a small sledge hammer just like the one I used on mama.

I told Hector "Tell me where the money is and this will be over." He yelled "I ain't got no money!" So I smashed his big toe. He screamed worse than I had ever heard anybody scream before, started shaking violently like Monster, and died.

Just like that the muthafucka was gone. The stress and the pain must have been too much for his heart and he just clocked right the fuck out. I had been wanting to kill his ass for so long that I was glad that he was gone but I couldn't display too much joy right now because it might give away my cover story.

I turned to Sly and said "I didn't know the muthafucka would die from a smashed toe!" He took the hammer out of my hand and said "I know but if that money is out there we need to get it. And here's the thing. I've tortured enough muthafuckas to know when one of them is telling the truth. He seemed to be genuinely confused about what the fuck was going on.

My problem is I believe you but I also believe him so the only one between you two who had access to the money was your mama. It appears to me that she might have played both of ya'll and kept it herself. She didn't have time to spend it all before you took her out. So where do you think she might have hidden the money?"

I said "It would have to still be somewhere in the house." Sly said "These boys are going to get rid of this muthafucka. You, me, and Rock are gonna go look for that money."

134

The whole time Laneesha was still outside waiting to make a play to free me. When the cats brought out the body bag with Hector she thought it might be me and put her head down and cried. But she also knew it could have been Hector because she saw them bring him in too so she continued to wait. They put the bag in the trunk and sped away.

A minute later Rock and me came out and he was leading me by the arm to the car. Sly lingered back a little to gather up my money bag and began making his way to the car. Just as me and Rock reached the car Laneesha snuck up quickly and fired one right in the back of his head.

When he fell, it knocked both of us to the ground; him on top of me. For some reason she didn't see Sly come out right behind us. As soon as Laneesha shot Rock Sly shot her with a .45 putting a big hole in her back.

She was on the ground wheezing as Sly stood over her to shoot her in the face. I grabbed Rocks gun and put one into the center of his forehead. He fell like a giant off a bean stalk smashing his face against the side of the car before he hit the ground.

I quickly crawled to Laneesha and got to hold her for about 30 seconds before she died. I yelled to her "Laneesha, I love you, please don't go!" She looked into my eyes and mouthed the words "I love you" just before her spirit left her body.

Seeing her die like that hurt bad and made me cry. I wanted to stay with her and cry longer but I knew I couldn't. The cops would be there any minute. I riffled Rock's and Sly's pockets, collected $7,000, grabbed up all the guns, put them in my bag with the $103k, jumped in Laneesha's car and sped away.

No time to morn right now because I have to act fast. Money is power and soldiers are power but soldiers cost money. The less money a man has the less likely he is to have power and without money they can't afford soldiers.

I couldn't continue to be in a situation where I had the streets and the cops after me; running and hiding from two enemies. I live and work in the streets. I need the ability to hide from the cops in the streets also. So I had to get to Sly's money to keep one of his soldiers from rising to power and coming after me.

Whoever got his money would get his power and the number one act to establish their supremacy would be to get me. In order to eliminate this threat I had to get his money quickly before news of his death got out.

I knew Sly never took his business anywhere near the home where his wife lived. I also knew that he had two other women besides his wife that he laid up with. Both of them lived in suburbs, one in Amherst and the other in Williamsville, not very far from each other.

One woman was kind of fat which is where he went when he wanted to eat and get a good night sleep. The other woman was really fine, which is where he went when he wanted to get a good fuck and sleep as well. You could look at her and tell her talent was not cooking.

I figured, since he was a veteran drug dealer, that he must have kept a getaway bag with both of his side pieces so I had to get those bags at all cost.

I went to the fat lady's house first and told her that Sly had just gotten into a shoot out with the cops and is lying low. He sent me since not too many people know me, under threat of death, to get his getaway bag. He told me to tell you that it is evidence that connects you to him so you have to get rid of it.

He also said to tell you that calling him will help the cops trace his location by the tower the signal pings off. He will use a burner to call you in a few days so if you see a strange number don't be afraid to answer it will be him.

She hurried up and got the bag and gave it to me saying "Here, take it, I don't want to get caught up in this mess." Then she said "wait". She went and got another bag, and said "take this one too. I can't have none of this shit here!" In the first bag was $300k but the second bag was the jackpot: 5 uncut kilos.

When I went to the fine lady's house I told her the same story but she gave me a hard time and questioned me. Finally, I had to play the young boy act and let a tear roll from my eye while saying "Don't you understand that if I don't get that bag to him in a hurry he is going to have that crazy muthafuckin Rock kill me! You had better start thinking about yourself because after they kill me they will come after you to kill you too."

She stared at me skeptically for a minute then turned, went in the back, and came back with the cash bag. If Sly had left drugs here too I had to get that also because it can be easily turned into money that can be used to come after me.

I said "I think he told me there were two bags?" She looked at me suspiciously, kind of sucked her teeth, went back in the back again and came back with the other bag. Bang, another jackpot, 5 more kilos. I said to myself "Yes!"

Again, playing the young boy role and just wanting to get to rub up against this fine muthafucka (who was wearing a low cut silk teddy with some real big pretty titties that looked like they were trying to climb out over the top to get a good look at me) I hugged her and said "thanks miss." Then I said you got some nice titties ma'am... you think I can..." She said "Get out of here boy!"

I grabbed the bags and dashed being happy that it all worked out the way I wanted. An enemy in the streets was eliminated and I finally got to get my revenge on that Hector muthafucka. No more pussy for you bitch! I started laughing and mimicking how he was shaking as he coded out.

After a good laugh I got my game face back on because I have to get out of the city in a hurry. Rock's boys know who I am and where I'm staying.

Within the next half hour I checked out of the hotel and paid the bill so that I wouldn't have any crime dogging my fake identity. I packed the wheel and tire wells of the trunk of my car with Sly's loot, ditched Laneesha's car, and hit the highway in search of a nice place to hide in plain sight where I had no connections.

Now I have the time and can afford to morn for Laneesha. She is the only person who I can truly say loved me unconditionally. Her loss is the first loss of my life that has really affected me deeply. I felt Mad Dog's loss but this is different. Her loss feels like something is missing from my own body.

Mama used to say that the newly dead can still hear you. So I said to Laneesha as if she was right next to me "I always said you weren't my girlfriend but you were. You were the best and truest girlfriend I ever had. Your life was hard ever since you were a little so rest in peace baby girl. I'll never stop loving you boo."

After a good long cry, I decided to take a slow ride down to Atlanta, Georgia while thinking back over some of the people I've met, the women I've had sex with, and things that happened in my life.

Chapter 9
JAISHA

"No man is worth your tears, but once you find one that is, he won't make you cry."
~ **William James**

Jaisha Ross, or Jah as she is called by her friends, is a very smart, pretty, and petit young girl. She stands about 5'2", weighs 110 pounds and looks like Sanaa Lathan coming toward you but Meghan Goode walking away. She is light skinned with soft naturally curly brown hair and a small amount of freckles across her nose and under her eyes.

Jah is a very popular girl at Bennett High School where she is Co-Captain of the Girls' Volleyball Team as well as Vice President of Student Government. She lives on Rounds Avenue, 5 houses down from Lashaun, and went to PS 80 with him and Sheila.

Lashaun has been having sex with Jah off and on since the 7th grade when he first moved into the neighborhood. She liked him back then and wanted him to be her boyfriend but Sheila got him. Jah believes that she could have had him but her mother didn't want her to see him. For some reason her mother never liked him.

Jah loves Lashaun and hates him at the same time. She knows that he is in love with Sheila but always appears acting cute and sweet when he wants to have sex with her.

Jah knows that she is only being used but she can't help it. She really loves how he makes love to her. Then she almost cannot stand the sight of him after they are done.

They have had a true love/hate relationship for about 5 years where they fight, argue and have fun together all at the same time. Once Lashaun begins to seduce her, though, she always gives in to him.

****

The day mama was bringing me home from Hopevale to my new house on Rounds Avenue we passed by a house where there was a very pretty girl sitting on the steps. I couldn't seem to take my eyes off of her ass we passed and I even turned around almost totally in my seat so I could continue to look at her. She kept looking in my direction too.

When I realized that my house was going to be just a few houses down the street from hers I got excited. I couldn't wait until I got a chance to meet her. That chance came sooner than I expected.

Apparently, she saw that we pulled into a driveway close by and decided to come down and introduce herself. When I pulled my bag out of the trunk and turned around she was just standing there behind me. She said "Hi, are you just moving in here?"

I tried to look at her but her head seemed to line up perfectly in front of the bright afternoon sun so I couldn't really see her face. I stepped to the side to turn away from the sun and finally I could see and she was truly a thing of beauty.

I said "Oh, wow, you are really pretty." She smiled and said "I'm Jaisha what's your name. I said "I'm Lashaun. Do you live down the street?" She said "Yes".

Just then mama yelled "Get in this house boy. You don't have time for socializing right now. Go away little girl!" Jaisha had a scared look on her face now. She said "Bye", turned and walked away real fast. I thought she was pretty and funny now and couldn't wait to see her again.

The next day came and I kept looking down the street to see if she had come outside. I didn't want to just knock on her door. What was I going to say some lame shit like "Can you come out and play?" No, I had to wait and make it look like we just bumped into each other.

Finally, she came out and sat on her front steps. I walked toward her house like I was on the way to the store or something but acting like I didn't notice her. She yelled "Where you going new boy?"

I said "Nowhere. Just talking a walk through the neighborhood to see what's around here. Since I am the "new boy" I gotta see where everything is." She said "Good, I'll come with!"

We had a good time walking through the neighborhood talking and enjoying the fresh summer morning air. She was like a tour guide showing me where important people lived, who was good to know, and who to avoid.

She seemed to want to warn me particularly about a kid named Wesley who also lived on Rounds but a couple of blocks up from us. She told me that Wesley and his teenaged crew did burglaries and sometimes robbed people in the area. He liked her but she couldn't stand him because he would try to bully her every now and then. For some reason I couldn't wait to meet this nigga to size him up.

That chance came on Halloween. Jaisha was like a big sister to all the little kids in the neighborhood and was taking a group of them around for trick-or-treat. When she saw me coming up the street she asked "Can you help me take these kids around and keep them safe? I heard Wesley and his boys are out taking little kid's candy." I said "Sure, no problem" being glad that she was really asking me to protect her."

We had hit our last stop and were coming out of Big Mike's Sub Shop when we spotted Wesley and two of his boys walking toward us. They were all just average size boys but I could tell they were stuck on stupid.

Wesley came up to me like he was tough and said "Give up the bags!" I said "Get outta here fool!" looking him in the eye and forcing him to look me in the eye so that he wouldn't notice me positioning my feet for a knockout punch. He said to his boys "Oh, we got a tough guy here."

As soon as he said that I hit him with a hard and fast left hook to the temple knowing that his head would fall. I followed that up with a hard and fast again under his chin with a right uppercut.

The boy folded up like luggage and went to sleep on the pavement. I took him down so quick his boys were stunned. They looked at each other and just ran away as fast as they could.

Jaisha kept saying "Oh, my god! Oh, my god!" I pulled her by the arm to get her to start thinking about getting these kids home. She said "Come on kids let's go home!"

Then she looked back at me and said "I can't believe you knocked him out!" I said "He had it coming. He shouldn't have been out trying to terrorize pretty ladies and little babies." She stared at me and smiled like she wanted to give me the pussy right then.

A couple of days later I would finally get the chance to get it. Jah helped me with my homework sometimes but we normally sat either on her porch or my porch. Whenever Jah's mother would see me on the porch with her she would make me leave. She would always say the same thing: "What do you want around her boy. Get off my porch and stay away from my daughter!"

Her mother didn't want her to let anyone in the house, especially me, while she wasn't home. Since it was now November Jah invited me to come inside anyway. Doing homework wasn't on her mind though.

She had room in the house with a large soft brown leather recliner in it. That room was her dad's den when he was alive. Her dad died about 5 years ago but her mom decided to keep his den just as he left it. Jah sat me down in the chair then sat down on top of and facing me.

We made love that day like two virgins just kissing, hugging and rubbing up against each other with our shirts off. We kept our pants on so there was no penetration but she dry humped me so good that she made me come. I think she came too once as she moaned deeply and shook like she was shivering while pulling my head down and burying my face between her titties.

From that day on, at least two or three times a week all through 7th grade, we would sit in that chair and make love without a care. After I met Sheila we still did it sometimes but not as often.

Several years passed and now we are juniors in high school. As I was walking home from track practice one day I spotted her fine, wanna be my baby mama ass, coming back from the corner store on Orleans.

"What's up baby girl?" I asked. "What's up with you baby boy" she replied. I asked her "Did you get me something from the store?" and tried to pull open the bag."

She snatched it away and said "No, I ain't even been thinkin about yo ass!" I said "Why, what did I do now?" She said "It's what you didn't do." I said "What?" She said "You know my Junior Prom is coming up and you still haven't asked to take me." I said

"What? I mean I, you…" "Yeah, yo ass is tongue tied now right? That's ok. You gonna want some of this pussy but you ain't gettin shit!" she said trying to look mean. I said "Hold up, Jah, I meant to ask you. I just forgot." I grabbed her by her waist and said "Can I take you to the prom baby?"

Jah pushed away from me, stepped back, and looked me up and down for a few seconds. Then she said "My gown is peach. Go to Tuxedo Junction in the Galleria I've already put your shit on reserve. Make sure they give you the right color" and she just walked away.

This girl was so bossy it was too funny. I liked how she knew what she wanted and just went for it.

Jah was going to be somebody important one day because the girl was smart, tough and a natural leader. People naturally responded to her and she could get them to do things even when they really didn't want to. Like me, I really didn't want to take her ass to the prom, but now I'll be taking her anyway.

I can see that she is going places and I know that her mother can see it too so she doesn't want me to fuck it up for her. The lady can't stand me and I understand why. She knows that her sweet little baby can't resist giving me that pussy. Her mom doesn't want what happened to her older sister to happen to Jah.

Jaisha has a sister who is about 7 years older named Melissa. Melissa had won all kinds of top honors in high school and received scholarships from 11 colleges around the nation. She earned a full ride at Johns Hopkins School of Medicine where she intended to study to become a doctor.

While there she met this guy who hung around campus. He wasn't even a student but he liked to hang around, party, and smoke weed with the college kids. He was a Black dude from Baltimore that wore dreads and pretended to be Jamaican or what I call Ja-fakin.

This cat managed to lead Melissa to believe that she didn't need college. When she dropped out of college he dropped two babies on her and then dropped her. To this day she is living in poverty, finds it hard to hold on to a job, and struggles every day to make ends meet. Her mom doesn't help her because she kept telling her to leave that fool alone but she just wouldn't.

I guess, like Jah with me, the girl couldn't help it. So, Jah's mom hates me with a passion. This is the reason I didn't want to ask her to go to the prom.

When she finds out I'm taking Jah to the prom she is going to flip!

The night I went to pick Jah up for the prom her mom was trippin. She said to Jah, right in front of me, "Out of all the boys who I know that wanted to take you to the prom, you had to pick this muthafucka!" And she told me about 5 times that she wanted Jah back in the house no later than 11. She also threatened me several times that I had better not make her come looking for me. I just kept saying "Yes ma'am, yes ma'am."

Jah thought that shit was funny. I told her "See, you knew your mom was going to trip on me but you had to make me do this any way." She said "Awww shut up, boy. You ain't bleedin or no shit. What you can't take a little heat?" Then she laughed at me. I said "Yeah, ok, you laughin but this shit ain't funny."

She pulled up her dress just then to show me that she wasn't wearing any panties. I was a little shocked at first then I said "Girl, where is your draws?" She laughed and said "I won't be needing any."

I said "You are really naked under there ain't you. You are so nasty, no, just freaky!" "Shut up boy!" she said laughing. I had fun teasing her all the way to the banquet hall that was out on Transit Road in Amherst.

When we arrived the place was nice. Jah and her prom committee had decorated it with black and silver balloons and streamers and a silver disco ball. I thought that was strange because their school colors are blue and orange. They also had two pictures of everyone in the junior class all over the walls; one as a freshman and one as a junior. I guess the idea was to get to see how everyone had grown. But it looked really nice.

As soon as we walked in the door a group of girls ran over to Jah all talking at the same time and screeching like dolphins or some shit making that high pitched sound that I hate. I couldn't tell what the hell they were saying but Jah seemed to speak their language.

They grabbed her and whisked her off into a backroom or bathroom or something. I didn't see her again for about fifteen minutes. That gave me a chance to crush the buffet cause I was starving.

We were having a good time dancing and partying. Me and some of the guys formed an air guitar band and started performing to the music like we were in a big time band. I was so in to it that I was losing track of time.

Jah came up to me and said "It's 10:15." I said "OK, we still have plenty of time." Then she said "Do you remember what I'm wearing?" I looked at her dress puzzled at first then I said "Oh, I remember what you are not wearing." She said "I thought you wanted to get some of this tonight?" I said "I do, let's get out of here!"

Now time is running out and I haven't thought of a place to go. I've got mama's car so she is at home. We can't go to Jah's house where we usually hit it before her mother gets home from work. Then I remembered my boy Mad Dog's parents are out of town. His house is just a few blocks away from ours.

I called him up and said "I gotta come over right away. Did your parents still go out of town?" He said "Yes, but..." I hung up on him because he was such a wuss at home; didn't want to break the rules and shit. When he opened the door I burst in and said "I need to use your room real quick!"

He said "What..." But I just grabbed Jah's hand and started running up the stairs. Jah waived to him as she was going past and said "Hi Larry!" giggling.

When we got up stairs I pushed Jah on the bed and started trying to take off all my clothes. She said "We don't have time for that boy!" She hiked up her dress and said "Just take your pants down."

I dropped my pants to the floor and now to get over to the bed I had to walk like Django in chains shuffling my feet and shit. I fell and hit the floor hard. Then I had to jump up and hop up onto the pussy like a paraplegic because my feet were all tangled up in my pants. Jah was laughing like crazy.

We got done and made it home with a couple minutes to spare. As she was getting out of the car Jah kissed me and said "I thought you were going to miss out on your prom night pussy." I said "I wouldn't have missed that for the world."

She said "You almost did" and started mocking the way I had to shuffle my feet like a slave. She said "You looked like Kunta Kinte with the club foot. "Iz comin Kizzie, Iz be right darre" cracking herself up. I said laughing "That shit ain't funny!" and drove away.

The end of the school year was approaching fast and Jah received an offer to go to China for a summer internship. A condition of the offer is that she would have to complete her senior year of college there as a foreign exchange student.

Then she would be offered a job with the Beijing Automotive Group in their New York City offices upon graduation. She was already able to speak Chinese Mandarin conversationally. So this was just the kind of opportunity that her mom had been preparing her for.

Jah came down to my house the day before she left for China which she rarely did because she was scared of my mother. She said "I have something to tell you." I said "You love me and are going to miss me?" She said "Nooooo nicka! playfully. I have to tell you that on prom night I became pregnant."

"Oh shit", I said backing up and sitting down on the stoop. "Is this going to fuck you up with going to China?" I asked. She said "No because I had an abortion. "You what?" I asked.

"That is what I had to tell you Jah said. I didn't want to tell you before because I couldn't allow you to be involved in a decision that was going to impact the rest of my life. If I had a baby right now it would have ruined me." She started crying and asked "Do you understand?"

I hugged her and said "Yes baby of course I understand." She said "It hurt me to do it but I had to. I had to." I said "I know and I'm sorry. If it wasn't for me…" She said "No, it wasn't you. It was me but I'm sorry I couldn't have the baby."

We sat on the stoop just holding each other without saying a word for about an hour. Then she stood up, kissed me, and walked away. She didn't say good-bye to me on the day she left so that was the last time I'd ever see her.

Chapter 10

RESA

*"The less you open your heart to others,
the more your heart suffers."*
~ Deepak Chopra

Resa Yvette Richardson is a gorgeous 17 year old Black girl whose grandfather was a full breed Seneca Indian that attends South Park High School. She is struggling trying to make it through school while working at night as a under aged stripper performing under the name Velvet.

Resa Looks a lot like Chaka Khan did when she was young. She is always draped in ivory, turquoise, and silver jewelry and wears her hair in two braids with a head band like an Indian squaw.

She is 5'5", 145, with a heavy backside, mocha latte colored skin, and big black baby eyes that reveal the depth of her soul. There is something penetrating about her eyes that make it hard to even look at her sometimes.

She is on welfare but working nights to make ends meet because at 17 she already has a 1 year old baby. I didn't know this at the time I met her but her baby is by a boy who plays on my football team; Ricky

Franklin. Ricky abandoned her after she got pregnant and began seeing other girls.

Now Resa picks boys to be with who Ricky knows to make him jealous hoping that he will come back to her. He does come back to her every now and then just to hit it but he runs off again without giving her the marriage and family type of commitment that she wants.

There is another guy on our team named Lashawn Jackson. Our team mates team tease us saying we are some sort of cross breed twins because we look like we could be brothers and we have similar names.

When I met Resa she was waiting for me one day after a game as I came out the stadium tunnel. She asked me "Is your name Lashawn?" I said "Yes, who are you?" The girl was fine and sweet looking so I was interested in her immediately.

She said "I watched you play today and wanted to meet you." As we talked she gave me the impression that she wanted to get with me. I took her home and dug that back out while mama was gone.

After we finished having sex and were getting dressed we were joking around with each other. Then she said something and right after that she said "Aint that right Mr. Jackson?" At first I thought she might have made a mistake but then I thought "Wait a minute."

I asked her "What did you call me?" She said "Mr. Jackson. Your name is Lashawn Jackson ain't it?" I laughed and said "No, I'm Lashaun Johnson." It turned out she thought that she was giving her pussy to another dude. It was so funny and I know that she had to be embarrassed.

I didn't care at the moment. I just got some pussy that was meant for another guy and that shit was really good so it was all good with me.

Ricky and Lashawn were kind of rivals because they often were competing for the same girls. I think Resa was trying to get with Lashawn to drive Ricky crazy and it back fired on her. But I didn't find out this part of the drama until after I took Resa to a party.

She was fine, very sexy, fun to be with, and the pussy was good so I figured that I could hang out with her for a while.

When I walked into the party with Resa holding her hand another cat I went to school with, Howard Exum or "X" as we called him, asked me "What are you doing with Ricky's lady?" I asked "Ricky who?" He said "Ricky Franklin. That's his baby's mama." "Oh shit, I said, she didn't tell me anything about Ricky." He said "Yeah, man, that's Rick's girl." I said "Thanks X, I'll handle this shit."

I grabbed Resa and told her that something came up and we had to go. She wanted to stay but I said "Nah, you are coming with me." I didn't say anything to her while taking her home. When I pulled up in front of her apartment she said

"Are you going to tell me what's going on?" I said "Let's go inside for a minute and I'll tell you." I wanted to get her alone just in case I had to go up side her head for tricking me and making me look stupid in front of my friends.

I asked her "Who is your baby's father?" She said "Ricky Franklin." I asked "The same Ricky Franklin that plays on my football team?" She said "Yes!" I tried to remain calm because I really didn't want to beat her ass although I really felt like it. I said "Don't you think that is something I should have been told? You got me going around acting like you are my woman and people are telling me that you are his woman!"

Then I asked her "Are you still seeing him?" She said "Yes." I asked her "Why?" She said "Because he is my daughter's father and I still love him." I asked her "Do you still sleep with him?" She said shyly "Yes."

Now I'm in a pickle where I have to make a choice. This girl is fine and that pussy is good so I don't want to give it up just yet. I asked her "Do you still want to be with me?" She said "Yes, I love him but I also love being with you."

So I told her "I love being with you too but here's the deal. If you get pregnant while you are still having sex with both of us, I don't have any responsibilities. Do you understand?" She said "Yes." To be sure I asked her "If you get pregnant whose baby will it be?" She said "Ricky's."

Now, guys can be like little bitches sometimes and they will turn against you if they think you been back stabbing one of the boys by fuckin his girl. So, I went to Ricky and told him what happened and that I didn't know she was his girl.

"I said "Listen, man, if you are still trying to be with her I will just step aside but I will take her if you don't want her." He said "Nah, man, you can have her. She ain't a bad girl and she's got a lot of love to give but I'm just done with her." I said "Cool, man, and dapped him up. I didn't want you to think that I was stabbing you in the back and going after your woman."

He said "Nah, bruh, it's cool. She's just my baby's mama that's all." I figured after talking with him man to man he might back off but then I found out that he was going behind my back and still fuckin her.

"That's cool, I thought to myself, I'm not gonna be a little bitch about it like they would." I will just keep hittin the pussy whenever I can but I won't be sporting her around like she was my lady anymore.

This actually worked out good for me anyway because I really didn't need the word of me being with Resa getting back to Sheila. She was my baby's mama and I truly loved her so I didn't want to piss her off.

Now I know that I can just have sex with Resa on the low and there will be no problems. I loved to hit that especially from the back. When she was really turned on her pussy would get bright red and swell up like a baboon's butt. But I liked hittin that monkey booty, smashing it hard, and turning her every way but loose.

Plus she was really good at suckin my dick with her pillow soft lips; slobbering and sucking on it like a peppermint stick. I thought that this was just going to be some good ass free pussy until Resa started wanting to see me exclusively.

She started acting like she was my girlfriend trying to question who I was with and where I had been. I exploded and asked her "You out here fuckin Ricky and you have the nerve to question me about who I'm with? You have got to be out of your rabbit ass mind!"

She said "I'm not seeing him anymore. I can't stand to be with him after being with you. The way you feel inside of me makes every cell in my body feel alive like electricity is flowing through me." I knew what she was saying was true because I felt the same thing too but I couldn't let her lock me down. I was in love with Sheila.

I had to go for the knockout punch to let her know without question that she couldn't lock me down. I told her "It's too late for us to be a couple. You was fuckin another dude and me at the same time so now you think I'm gonna want you?

I'm in love with Sheila. You are nothing more than a period piece to me. You are just a piece that I come to get when Sheila is on her period.

What makes you think that after I know you been hittin another nigga and me that I would want to see you exclusively?"

She shouted "Because I'm pregnant and I know that it's yours!" I was shocked for a second but I said "Get the fuck outta here with that shit! You fuckin two dudes at the same time and you gonna try to tell me that it's mine. Bitch, please!"

She said "I know it's yours. As soon as you came into me one day I felt something move inside me and I knew right then that I was pregnant. I just waited until I missed my period to confirm it but baby I knew it right then.

That was the same day I grabbed your dick and held it close to me like it was a baby." I remember that and I wondered what the fuck she was doing.

I said "Do you remember the conversation that we had when you first told me that you were still fuckin Ricky?" She said "Yes." "What did we agree" I asked. She said "If I get pregnant, you don't have any responsibilities." I said "That's right now whose baby is it?" She started crying and said "Ricky's!" I said "You damn right" and walked out.

I was trying to get away from her but Resa would still call my house and show up unannounced all the time especially after she started getting bigger. She told me Ricky was saying it wasn't his baby either and had stopped seeing her or coming by to see his baby. I felt sorry for her in a way but I already had one baby to take care of and couldn't afford to take care of two.

Mama would get mad at me asking what I was doing to that girl and if that was my baby. I had to tell mama the whole story and that the girl was just trying to get me to support her. She couldn't work at the strip club anymore so she needed extra cash. She knew that I was a gambler and a hustler so I thought she figured me for an easy mark.

Ricky didn't do anything but play football and video games and wasn't supporting his baby. I wasn't about to be feedin both of his little muthafuckas. Nah, I was born at night but it wasn't last night.

Mama said "Well, you better do something to get rid of her ass then cause I don't want her to keep coming around here."

By this time Resa was almost 7 months pregnant. I went to her apartment and told her that mama didn't want her coming by or calling to the house anymore. She started crying and screaming "Why, this is your baby!"

I said "Listen, bitch, I thought we already settled this shit. That muthafucka ain't mine! You ain't gonna have me takin care of some other nigga's shit. You think I fuckin stupid? That's it. You think I'm stupid because you been playin me from the start! If you

162

ever open your mouth and say that's my baby again, I will fuck you up!"

"It is your baby!" she screamed. Before I knew it I back handed her across the face so hard that she flew over and kind of disappeared behind this arm chair. I threw the chair out of the way to get to her and when I grabbed her up she had a lot of blood in her mouth.

She started screaming while holding her stomach "My baby, my baby!" She pushed away from me and ran in the bathroom. I could hear her in there crying and screaming then she yelled "It's coming out. The baby is coming out!"

I pushed open the door and saw that she had this 2 or 3 pound bloody mess in her hands. I saw it move a little bit but I told her "That thing is dead you better get rid of it." She said "No, it's a baby." I grabbed her by the neck, squeezed hard, and said "Flush that shit!"

She threw it in the toilet and flushed but it didn't go down. I ran in the kitchen, got a butcher knife, handed it to her and said "Cut it in half." She started crying really loud so I snatched her by the hair and yelled in her face "Cut it bitch!" Resa cut it and flushed then it was gone.

She was still bloody and crying so she had to be cleaned up. I filled the bathtub with water just enough to come up to her waist. I had seen the birth of babies on TV and knew that she still had to deliver the afterbirth.

I sat her in the hot tub, washed her up, and washed her hair. After she delivered the afterbirth, I chopped it up and flushed it. Then I carried her into the bedroom, dried her off good, and put her to bed.

I never saw Resa again after that day. The truth is I didn't want to see her anymore. But I heard from one of Ricky's friends that she moved out of town shortly after she lost the baby.

I also heard that he was bragging to his boys that he had dodged a bullet by her having a miscarriage. I was mad as hell because I had to take care of the shit he wasn't man enough to handle.

I thought about ambushing and executing his muthafuckin ass. "Star high school football player shot and killed. We'll have a live report from the scene on News at 11!" I imagined hearing the headline on TV. But then I thought better and said "I'll let that stupid muthafucka live."

Now, life has a way of delivering odd or sometimes cruel coincidences. There was a young lady that hung out in the gambling joint named Debbie. She was about 5 years older than me and very sexy. I knew that she knew Resa because I would see them talking and laughing together sometimes after Resa performed but what I didn't know until later that she was Resa's older sister.

I never went around Resa's family. I accidently met her mother when I bumped into them while they were out shopping one day. I knew that she had an older sister, who she called Deeba.

Deeba was Resa's nickname for Deborah because when she was a baby Resa couldn't say Deborah but would say "Deeba" instead. Apparently, the nickname stuck but it was only used within the family. Deborah went by her real name or Debbie outside of the family.

A few weeks after last seeing Resa, I struck up a conversation with Debbie in the joint and we started hitting it off good. She liked to dance and kept me dancing with her all night. I found out later that she was dating the DJ and they were having trouble because he was seeing other women.

She was dancing, having fun, and playing sexy with me in front of him to make him jealous. But he was actually done with her and ignoring her attempts to make him jealous because she was crazy. She was fine and sexy but certifiably psycho. He was happy to see her with another dude so that maybe she would stop stalking him.

He drove a red corvette which she knew he loved so she would attack it. She would do the most damage to it after she saw him with another woman in it. This crazy woman slashed his tires on several occasions, scratched the paint, broke windows, ripped off his windshield wipers and would have poured sugar in his gas tank but luckily he had it locked. So she cracked eggs all over the car and then poured the sugar over the eggs so it would bake under the hot sun.

The cat called the police on her many times for breaking into his house. If she thought he had a girl inside, she would climb into the house through the basement window to see who it was. But she always managed to escape before the cops came.

One time he came home and found her in there and tried to force her to leave. When he started calling the cops she stripped off all of her clothes thinking they wouldn't make her leave if she was naked. Instead of pressing criminal charges they took her butt naked ass to the hospital for a mental evaluation.

Here is the thing I kind of like about crazy women. For some reason they have some really good ass pussy. Maybe because they don't hold back or because they don't care what people think they will do anything sexually.

They will do things normal women might be afraid to do because they think it might make them look like a slut. But crazy women don't care so they will give up that pussy any way, anytime and anywhere.

The first day I hit it she had me stand up against the wall. Then she did a hand stand in front of me turned around and backed up walking in her hands so that now her coochie was near my face. Next she slid her hips down to line up her pussy with my dick and gripped the sides of my hips with her knees.

Once I slid my dick between those warm wet lips she started twerkin that ass like mad. The sight of her ass moving like that swallowing up my dick and the way it felt with her popping and grinding on me made me come quickly.

The next time we did it she had me sit on the couch. She sat on me facing me then put her feet next to my hips. She grabbed onto the back of the couch and started bobbing up in down on my dick like a cowboy riding a horse he is trying to break.

She sat down after that spreading her legs in a complete split, grabbed the back of my neck pulling my face into her chest, and bobbed up and down. She made my dick so hard it felt like steel. As she was rolling and grinding on me it seemed as if the lips on her pussy were like wet lips gently kissing my nuts.

I knew that I was about to come in a few minutes and I wanted to bang this nut out. So I tried lay her on her back length wise on the couch but she wanted her head to be toward the back of the couch. When I put her in that position she locked her feet behind her head giving me total access to the pussy.

I banged out that nut slamming hard, fast and deep into the pussy to the point where she made me scream: "Damn this pussy is good!" She said "You really like this pussy daddy?" I said "Hell yeah I like this pussy and I better not catch you giving it to anybody else." She said "I won't daddy. This pussy ain't nobody's but yours now."

We were laying in bed one Saturday afternoon after waking up from a triple header and Deborah started talking about her sister. The more she talked about her the more I started to think she was talking about Resa. I asked her "What is your sister's name?" She said "Resa."

I jumped up and starting putting on my clothes real quick. She asked me "What are you doing; where are you going?" At first I didn't say anything to her and just kept getting dressed.

As I was putting on my jacket she grabbed the sleeve to stop me and asked "What's wrong? Why are you leaving?" I said "I had no idea that Resa was your sister. I used to date her." She said "Get the fuck outta here. You got to be kidding." I said "Nope, if I knew, I never would have messed with you.

"You're not the one that made her have an abortion are you?" she asked. I said "I didn't make her have an abortion but I was with her when she miscarried."

She said "Abortion, miscarry, you know what I'm talkin bout nigga! You beat her ass and made her lose that baby didn't you?" I said "That ain't the way it happened." She said "Nah, nigga that's just the way it happened. You need to pay for that shit."

She got up and walked out of the room and I dashed out of the door. I wasn't about to wait around to see what she had on her mind.

Almost an hour after I got home this crazy chick came to my house and broke in. There were three small panes of glass in the upper part of the front door. She broke one and reached her hand in to undo the lock. She did not realize that my mama was home.

Mama had a collection of porcelain dolls that she kept on display on a table near the door. When Deborah opened the door and poked her head in mama smashed her upside the head with one of those dolls shattering it but knocking her out. Deborah had a big butcher knife with her that went sliding across the floor.

Mama had tied her hands behind her back and used a belt to secure her by her neck to the base of the banister leading upstairs. Mama had a pearl handle .22 revolver that she carried to protect herself from Leroy and she was pointing it in Deborah's face when she came to.

Crazy people are always doing shit to terrorize other people but they never want anybody to do anything to them. When she realized that she was tied and saw the gun she began to plead with mama "Please don't kill me. Please don't kill me!"

Mama said "I have every legal right to kill you. You broke in my house while holding a deadly weapon. There is no jury on the planet that would convict me of killing your bitch ass right here. But here is what I'm gonna do. I am going to have the cops deal with your ass since you committed 3 felonies you gonna do at least 20 years."

Deborah started crying and pleading real hard now. The one thing she was most afraid of was going to prison. The thing she was afraid of the most after prison was Laneesha. She knew that chick was much more crazier than her and she would not hesitate to put her down.

She pleaded with mama "Please, I'm sorry, I will never do this again. You will never see me again!" I told her "You are right. She will never see you again because I am going to have Laneesha come and see you."

Deborah's eyes got real big, she stopped crying, her voice got real calm, and she said "Ok, I lost my mind for a minute. I never should have come over here. I can't fuck with ya'll cause ya'll on a whole other level of shit.

Please ma'am. I will never bother you or your son ever again." I said "You know all I have to do is give the word to Laneesha and you will be taking a dirt nap right?" She said "Yes. I'm not fucking around with ya'll anymore."

When she said that mama pushed her head up against the banister hard, stuck the barrel of the gun in her eye, cocked it, and said "If you ever come over here again, this bullet right here will be waiting for you." Deborah started crying again and said "Ok, I won't. I promise I won't!"

Mama took Deborah's knife, cut her hands loose, unbuckled the belt, and let her go. Then mama warned me "Don't you ever bring no shit like this to my house again." "Yes mama. Thank you for coming to my rescue." I said. Then mama said laughing "One thing is for sure. At least that bitch ain't gonna come to my house anymore!"

That was the last I ever saw of Deborah. I guess when crazy has to face crazier they start realizing that they ain't really that crazy.

The girl upped and disappeared. Maybe she moved out of town with her sister because I never saw her anywhere. She never came to the joint again after that either.

I was glad of that because ladies with pussy as good as Deborah's can seduce a half ass hazardous muthafucka to murder a mug for her just to keep getting that shit. I was so glad she was gone because I didn't want to have to watch my back on the street like that.

Chapter 11

Carol

*"Love doesn't claim possession,
but gives freedom."*
~ Rabindranath Tagore

A week before I was released from prison I was visited by my Probation Officer: Terrance Kent. He was a tall, thin, light skinned, curly haired Terrance Howard lookin cat.

"My job, he said, is to put you back in here after you get out. The reason you will end up back in here is for one of two reasons: you will either think the rules of probation don't apply to you or you will fail to make a plan to stay out of here. Those who don't make a plan to stay out of here are right back in here before they know it.

If you fail to plan, you are planning to fail. So, if you don't want to come back in here I suggest that over the next week before your release you make yourself a plan. Otherwise, you should ask the CO's to hold your cell and hold your job because you will be right back.

You will report to me within 3 weeks of your release and you had better have a job and a permanent residence by then. No job, no permanent residence and you're back here for the next 3 years.

You will be randomly drug tested whenever I feel like it and if you come up positive, you will be right back in here. I will inspect your residence randomly also to make sure that you are not engaging in criminal activity and that you are keeping your curfew. Get caught breaking curfew or with contraband and you will be right back here.

Understand that I am not your buddy or your friend. If you lie and try to bullshit me like I'm your mama or somebody who usually lets you get away with shit, I will bounce your ass right back in here. So do yourself a favor. If you don't wanna be in here 3 more years, make yourself a plan."

"Finally, he said, since you are young I am going to give you a bit of fatherly advice. The truth is I hope you never come back here but if you fuck up I will drop kick your ass back over these walls like a fuckin football. So don't get it twisted. The advice I am going to give you is this:

Along with failing to make a plan to stay out most young guys wind up back in here because they allow themselves to be framed. In my business, perception is reality. When people look like they are doing wrong they usually are. So don't give me the perception that you are doing wrong.

Not only to you have to present me with a good picture of yourself, you also have to present a good frame. Your frame is the people, places, activities and things that you surround yourself with.

When you are trying to show a picture of yourself to the world that picture is modified by a frame. No matter how you dress yourself up and try to present a good image in the picture the frame tells a different story or modifies the picture.

If you are trying to present to the world that you have changed or that you are a good guy, but the people you hang with, the places you go, the activities you engage in and the things that you do are NOT good, it will be difficult for people to actually see you as good.

Your frame not only influences how people see you it also influences the things you do and the trouble you get into. For the most part, young guys like you who end up in here were always with a "friend" when they got into trouble.

So, do yourself a favor. Make a plan, change your frame, and you will put yourself way ahead of the game of keeping yourself out of here. Capisci?" "Yes sir" I said.

Like Chris Rock dropping the mic he just got up and walked out. I sat there for a minute thinking about what he said and taking what he said seriously because I couldn't see myself doing 3 more years in this muthafucka. I was ready to get out and to stay out so I started making my plan.

There was a restaurant that I worked at before getting locked up. The lady who owned the place liked me so I figured that she would give me a job. I figured that mama would let me come back home but I didn't know how cool she would be with the Probation Officer coming by the house randomly.

She liked men in authority and PO Kent was a nice looking guy so I figured that she might try to give this nigga some pussy. If she did and he turned her down flat, she would get mad at me and make me get out so that she wouldn't have to see him again. Either way I knew that I had to get myself together, get a job, and earn enough money quick to be able to support myself.

I wrote mama the day PO Kent came and informed her of my release date. To my surprise, on that day, she was outside waiting to take me home.

My mama was not a very affectionate woman but every now and then she would do things to show me that she loved me. She never paid one visit or sent any commissary gifts while I was locked up. Being curious I had to ask her how she could have left me in there alone.

She said "You were not alone. You were where you chose to be with the people you chose to be with. When you do crime with the possibility of going to prison you are choosing to be with prisoners. I am your only family but you chose to leave me and be with your prison family.

Life is nothing but a series of choices. When you make a choice you have to deal with the consequence. You made the choice of leaving me so you had to deal with the consequence of not being able to see me."

"Plus, she said, I didn't want to do anything that would give you the impression that I supported you in your criminal activities. Visiting you and sending you things to make you more comfortable while in there is like me giving you approval to be there.

I want you to know in no uncertain terms that I am pissed off that you were out here committing crime and that you wound up in prison. You need to know that if you go back you will never see me again.

I didn't carry you nine months and go through several hours of painful labor giving birth to you for you to grow up to be a criminal or to be using a gun to hurt some other mother's son. I am not going to be one of those mothers who make excuses for their son. So, if you want help staying out, I will help you to stay out of prison. But just know that if you go back in, you will never see me again."

"Wow mama, I said, I had no idea you felt that way but I am going to do my best to respect the way you feel." We rode the rest of the way home without saying another word to each other.

When I entered the house I could tell mama had already cooked a meal for me. She knew I liked pot roast and mashed potatoes. She had that already cooked and being kept warm along with some green peas, crescent rolls, and red Kool-Aid with German chocolate cake. I ate like a pig that day and slept like a baby that night. It felt so good to be home.

Strangely, though, I began thinking about Jasmine and was starting to miss her. Before going to sleep I was thinking about ways to find her to see what it would be like to be with her outside of Wende's walls.

Then I suddenly remembered that I had beaten the shit out of her. Seeing her again, knowing how she is, wasn't even a possibility.

Before going to prison I used to work in a small restaurant called Carol's Kitchen near my old boyhood neighborhood off Walden near Bailey. It was owned by this fine ass older lady named Carol Winston. I got up the next day and went there to see if Carol would give me my old job back. I knew the lady liked me and figured that I could just about walk back in.

When I entered the door Carol's back was turned to me as she was serving a customer. "Hi Carol", I said. She turned around and looked at me for a few seconds and said "Oh, Hi Lashaun. How are you doing?" I said "Good, how are things going here?" She said "It's going good. What can I get for you?" I said "I was hoping that you could give me a job." "A job?" she asked in a surprised tone of voice.

She said "When you did have a job here you rarely showed up when you were supposed to and was late many times too. I got the feeling that you only wanted to say you had a job for some reason but you didn't really want to work. No, I'm not going to put up with anymore of that nonsense.

There are too many people who really want to work. They really have to earn to eat not just to disguise the money they are getting through criminal activity. Nope, I'm sorry, no job here honey." Then she walked away from me and started wiping down the lunch counter.

I was shocked that she read me like that. There is an old saying that the truth will set you free. I figured that if the truth could set you free, it could also keep you free. I needed a job to remain free from prison so I decided to tell her the truth.

I pleaded with her "Carol, I'm in a situation now where I have to earn to eat as well as to remain free." She suddenly stopped wiping the counter and asked "What does that mean?" I told her the whole story about being in prison and that I needed a job to keep from having to do 3 additional years locked up.

I could see her softening up a little so I begged a bit harder and said "You were exactly right about how I behaved working here before. But I am older now, have learned to accept more responsibility, plus I need to have this job in order to remain free.

My probation officer told me very directly that if I don't have a job within 3 weeks I was going back in. So, please give me a chance to prove that I have changed. The first day that I don't show up or am late you can fire me."

Carol still seemed to be hesitating about giving me the job so I told her about my experience working in the mess hall. I told her how I had learned everything about cooking and how to do it fast: from making mass meals for thousands of inmates, to short order cooking, to banquet style cooking for the Warden, CO's and their guests during their awards and decorations events.

Finally, she said "Ok, I will give you a chance based on your own standard. If you miss just one day or show up late just one day, don't bother coming back and don't make me have to ask you to leave. Do you understand?" she said sounding just like Jasmine.

I said "Yes ma'am! When do you want me to start?" She said "5:30 in the morning, every morning, she emphasized, I am going to start you on breakfast learning how we do it here from Lee. Don't disappoint me!"

I hugged her quickly and said excitedly "Thank-you, thank-you!" She laughed and said "Get away from me boy. See you tomorrow."

****

Carol Winston is a middle aged woman that serves fresh baked biscuits everyday but she also has hot buns. Carol is 48 but looks more like 38 and very well preserved. She is 5'7", 153, with honey blond shoulder length hair and looks more like Mariah Carey

180

than Mariah Carey. She is small in the waist and cute in the face and fine enough to attract a man of any taste.

Carol has a thing for young men. Many men in their 50's and 60's try to woo her constantly but she is not into older men. She says they just want somebody to be a maid and to cook and clean for them. She has tried a few of them over the years but in the bedroom they can't throw down how she likes to get down.

Unbeknownst to Lashaun Carol had her eyes on him when he worked for her before. She talked herself out of approaching him back then because of his age. Now, she sees that he is older, bigger, and stronger with prison muscles so now she is really interested in seeing how he will perform for her sexually.

****

Once I started working for Carol again I noticed that her husband, who she was legally separated from, was taking her for all he could. He was the cleanest, big car driving, non-working nigga I had ever seen because he was taking her money.

Every now and then he would come to the restaurant and sweet talk her into giving him money. Sometimes he would just go to the register and take it. Each time he did that it would make her cry because he would either hit or choke her and say some kind of vile shit to her before he stole the money.

In some ways, because of the way he acted and because he had very light skin with slicked back hair, he reminded me of Hector. I had it in my mind that I was going to fuck this muthafucka up one day. I didn't want to do anything to go back to prison but I wanted to get in his ass real bad.

He came in just about every week so I was going to get his ass next time he pulled this bullshit because I had started getting hot for Carol. She was about my mother's age but really fine for a older lady and I wanted to see what it would be like to hit that.

One day after closing as I was moping the dining room floor Carol came and sat on one of the tables and just watched me. I didn't notice what she was doing at first until she asked me "How old are you?" I stopped and said "19".

She stood up and said "Oh my Lord, you are still a baby but you do look like you almost a man." I said "I may only be only 19 but I'm all man."

She laughed and said "Boy, I ain't gonna fool with you." I laughed and started mopping the floor again but said to myself "You keep on, I'm gonna be gettin' some of that pussy from you."

About a week later just before closing her muthafuckin husband comes in again, chokes her up, threw her to the floor, took the money and started to leave. When he walked past me I hit him over the back with a chair and stomped on his face trying to break his nose.

As I was stomping him I said "You better not ever come back in here muthafucka or the next ass whuppin is going to be worse."

Then from the back of my pants I pulled out a fake Glock 9, which was really a BB gun but looked like a real gun, and pushed it into his face under his left eye. I said "Remember nigga, don't ever come back here again!" He tried to stand up to walk out but I kicked him in the head again and made him crawl out.

I went to see if Carol was alright but she was still lying on the floor crying. I tried to stand her up but managed to get her to sit in a chair. Feeling kind of bad for her I hugged her by pulling her head to my stomach.

She put her arms around my waist and before letting go she slid her hands down my butt cheeks and gripped the backs of my thighs with both hands.

Then she looked up at me and said "I'm ok now." I asked "Are you sure?" She stood up and said "Yeah, I'm sure." She gave me a little peck on the lips said "Thanks" and walked back into the kitchen.

Carol gave me a ride home that night after work. When I saw mama's car was gone I asked her to come in for a minute because I wanted to see if she would let me hit that ass real quick.

As soon as I closed the door I pushed her against the wall and gave her a long passionate kiss. When I saw that she was really getting into the kiss I slid her dress up and pulled her panties down just below her pussy.

I kept kissing her, not giving her much of a chance to breathe, as I inserted two of my fingers into her pussy which is now really wet and I began massaging her clit with my thumb.

I felt her clit was getting real fat so I kneeled down quick and began sucking and licking on it greedily while squeezing her booty and pulling that pussy into my lips and trying to get all of it my mouth.

She was moaning loud and her legs were shaking like she couldn't stand up anymore. I picked her up, laid her on the couch, and started digging her back out.

We were on the couch not more than 5 minutes when I saw the head lights of mama's car come through the front window and heard the sound of her car enter the driveway. I scrambled to help Carol get all of her clothes, slipped her out the backdoor, and ran upstairs to my bedroom.

That night I had a dream that I had finished fucking Carol and it was good. I could not wait until I got another opportunity to get into that pussy.

When I went to work the next day Carol was mad at me, first, for leading her to let me hit it in another woman's house. Second, she was angry for having to hide and sneak out. I knew that something was wrong because she was short with me all day. She waited until it was just me and her left there at the end of the day to tell me what she had to say.

"I'm not a high school girl, she said, don't lure me into your mama's house again. As a woman I would be mortified to catch another grown woman in my house with my son. Part of it is my fault because I should have known you would be living with your mama. At the same time when you asked me to come in you should have told me what the deal was. Don't ever put me in that kind of position again."

I understood what she was saying. At the same time though I was decoding it or reading between the lines because I wanted to hit that some more.

"Don't put me in that kind of position again" meant to me that I would have another opportunity to get her into position again. "Yes, oooo I can't wait to get to really hit that!" I said to myself in my head.

Instead of trying to explain or justify our actions in this situation, which only makes women angrier about whatever they are angry about, guys should just apologize. So I apologized, kissed her on the cheek, said it won't happen again, and then walked away.

All I had to do now is wait for the next opportunity. If she wanted me to hit it, she would lure me into a situation that was good for her.

I was surprised at the situation she chose for our next sex session. She chose to do it in her office.

Carol was in the office organizing receipts when I went in to dump her trash can. I was wearing a t-shirt

185

that was a little tight around my arms. She looked at me and said "You have some nice biceps."

Then she backed me up against the file cabinets and ran her fingers under my shirt rubbing my abs. I grabbed her by the back of her hair and tried to smother her with a passionate kiss. While I was kissing her she started undoing my pants.

She dropped down and started making love to my dick so good it was making my toes curl in my shoes. I started thinking about the number of women I've been with that gave amazing head and saying to myself "Is there a school or something where these muthafuckas go to learn how to do this shit."

She was doing it so good I knew that she would make me come and I didn't want to come right then. I scooped her up by her ass pulling up her dress at the same time and sat her on the desk.

When I buried my face between her legs I could feel the heat coming from that pussy. I was French kissing the lips around her clit like they were the lips on her face.

I stuck my thumb in her pussy and moved it in and out while sucking on her clit that was now swollen and standing at attention like a soldier. Carol came and screamed so loud I thought she might wake up the dead.

I scooped her up again and put her up against the wall this time and banged it out as hard and fast as I could while kissing her in a way that would take her breath away. She came again just before I came.

Feeling a little weak at this time I put her down but she grabbed my dick and kept pulling it toward her. At the same time she was slowly sucking one of my nipples.

It felt so good the way she kept stroking on my dick. I pulled her head back to give her a kiss but her hair was covering her face. When I moved her hair away and looked at her face she looked like she was drunk. I had never seen the look of total ecstasy before but this had to be it.

When I started kissing her she grabbed me by the back of my neck to keep her lips in contact with mine and pulled me over to her desk by my neck and my dick. She turned me around, laid me down, and hopped on top.

That pussy was hungry and swallowed my dick up. She was popping her hips and grinding in an alternating way that sent me into ecstasy.

Oh my god, this woman was really workin that ass. She made her butt cheeks clap better than any stripper I had ever seen and was making my dick do tricks inside her pussy.

It seemed like she was making herself come about every 5 minutes or so. She had to be damn near dehydrated from all of body fluid she lost because she had me soaked. I heard that women her age were dry and had to use lubrication but not Carol. She was just as hot and wet as any young girl that I had ever met.

From then on, every time I got a chance to have sex with Carol, I tried to fuck the shit out of her. But she stopped me one day and taught me a good lesson.

She said "Sometimes a woman wants a man to pull her hair back and just fuck the shit out of her. Most of the time, though, a woman who is in love or really likes a man wants him to make love to her. She wants her man to take his time and, like giving a personal massage, concentrate on lovingly administering pleasure to her body.

Mechanically, after so many strokes, a man is going to get off so love making is not really about delivering pleasure to him. Love making for the woman.

It is a mental process of engaging in love making that produces waves of orgasms, peaks and valleys, highs and lows, during the love making session.

When a woman wants her man to try to dig down to China through her vagina her orgasms are also mechanical. But most of the time she wants orgasms that are stimulated through her mind not her behind.

Women who are in bad or toxic relationships although they will still have sex with the guy they don't come so much. To most men a woman's orgasm is a prize that they think they earned because of what they did to her.

When a woman comes with a man it is not so much what he is doing to her more than how she thinks and feels about him. If you make a woman think and feel good about you, she will always come for you.

I come a lot with you because most of the time you don't make having sex feel like it's just about you. You seem to want me to get off too. That makes me feel good when I'm having sex with you so I come for you."

Carol taught me how to go beyond just fucking to making love. I thought fucking was making love but she showed me the difference and I could actually feel it.

I grew to love making love to her and missed sleeping with her sometimes when she couldn't be with me due to trips her husband was still putting her through.

I wanted to handle that muthafucka once and for all but she wouldn't let me as her way of protecting me from going back to prison. But I wanted to get his ass bad because although they were still married she was my woman. Fucking with her was like fucking with me but she made me promise not to interfere.

In this way she taught me how to regulate my emotion in volatile situations. She reminded me of that old Sicilian mafia credo: "Revenge is a meal best served cold."

Carol also taught me a lot about business and she especially taught me a lot about money. The first lesson she taught me about money I had never heard from anybody. It was confusing at first because I had no knowledge about anything spiritual.

She said "If you don't understand what I'm about to tell you about money you will never have any. If you ever get a large amount of money, without understanding this, you will never be able to keep it.

Our physical world was created by spiritual power. The force that animates our physical body and gives it life is spiritual power. There is a physical side to life and there is the spiritual side; physical power and spiritual power. Spiritual power is designed to amplify physical power; it is a force multiplier.

Those who plan to make a lot of money and become wealthy must learn to combine spiritual power with physical power.

There is a difference between being rich and being wealthy. You can work hard using physical power and get rich but if you apply spiritual power to physical efforts, you can become wealthy.

Using physical effort to make money without applying spiritual power is like trying to fight a multi-million dollar prize fight against a professional fighter with one arm tied behind your back.

You will work very hard, take a lot of lumps, and it will still be impossible to win the prize. If you understand how to apply spiritual power to your physical effort you'll always win.

Wealth is a manifestation of the application of spiritual power and principles to our physical money making efforts. 1% of the people in this country own 80% of the wealth. What are they doing differently than the other 99%?

The 99% also want to be wealthy? So why are they having difficulty becoming as wealthy as the 1%? The 1% understands how to apply spiritual power and principles to their physical effort.

If you try to use this information to get rich quick, it is not going to work. This knowledge is for those who know how wealth naturally grows.

People who get huge amounts of cash suddenly without this knowledge often lose it suddenly. Sometimes their lives are also ruined in the process. It is possible to get a load of cash quickly if you understand how the power and principles of wealth acquisition work and put them to work.

However, if you have this knowledge, you are less likely to lose that money suddenly. And you will know how to use cash properly so that it does not injure or ruin you. This type of knowledge gives life to all who find it and health to all their flesh. It will lend you the vitality you need to enjoy being wealthy."

I had never heard anything like this before but it made so much sense to me. For some reason the meaning and truth of it seemed to speak directly to something on the inside of me.

This may sound crazy but it felt like something that I always knew but didn't know. It was a truth that I just connected with immediately and in a way it changed me mentally.

From that day I began to think differently about making money. I now knew exactly why I had committed so many robberies but still didn't have any money.

Now nobody had to explain to me anymore why I didn't have shit. I had no spiritual knowledge about money, neither did mama, so it fled from her and me and kept us living in poverty.

A couple of days or so later Carol taught me another lesson about money that also impacted me greatly. It was a truth that seemed so true that I felt I had to take it and do something with it immediately. She said:

"The words money, cash and currency are used like they are the same but are actually three different things. We call that paper and coins we fold up and put into our pocket or purse money but it is not money. It is cash.

Contrary to popular belief money is not a thing. Cash is a thing. Money is an idea generated by spiritual energy that when put to work properly creates cash.

192

When spiritual energy takes the form of an idea with the potential to produce wealth it becomes money. The energy produced as a result of that idea is where the power lies to manifest that idea into physical forms and create cash.

That energy or money moves about and touches the minds of those holding the currency required to turn the money into cash.

Currency is the unique collection of inherent knowledge, gifts, talents and abilities that we all possess which have value that can be traded for cash and are used to turn ideas into cash.

Every one of us has currency. It was given by GOD when we were born as a type of birthday present. Cash is simply an extension or an expression of the value of money and currency.

Each person or market will project value onto money and currency based on how bad they want it or according to what others in the market are willing to pay for it. When you use money and currency to create value, the market naturally responds with cash.

Money is spiritual energy so it contains a lot of power. Money and women are very similar. Women are built to house a great deal of spiritual power. If a man cannot manage money properly, he will not be able to keep a powerful woman.

It is a well known fact that poor family financial management can lead to divorce. But most people don't know that money is also the spiritual force that drives a couple to divorce.

Money is a commodity. Men and husbands must understand that a woman is a commodity too who is equipped to make them wealthy. A woman and money MUST be utilized properly or they will both either leave a man for another man or cause a man to be ruined financially.

Money is a living entity. When it is used properly it produces wealth. Money must be allowed to do what it is designed by GOD to do. Otherwise, it will either go rotten on you or leave you.

Money always seeks to go to the man who knows how to utilize and appreciate it; to make it prosper or increase in value. A powerful woman is the same way.

She is always seeking the man who appreciates her and understands how to utilize her power to lead them both to prosper. If a powerful woman isn't appreciated or used properly, she will either go rotten on you or leave you.

When a powerful woman marries a man that turns out to be weak, she will leave him for one who is strong. You can't stop it. It is going to happen because there is a spiritual force driving all things in the universe toward maximum productivity.

A strong man understands the value of powerful woman. A strong man understands that his duties in a family are to guide, guard and govern; direct, correct and protect. So he keeps his woman close to him to constantly guide and direct her power in a way that causes them both to prosper.

A weak man is not strong enough to keep a powerful woman close so she gets away. Then he has to watch another man enjoy and become wealthy with a woman he wasn't strong enough to appreciate."

That day I began looking at Carol in a whole different way. She was not just a older lady who was good to have sex with. She was in my mind now a woman of great value.

I knew right then just how big of a fool her husband was. He would rather steal chump change from her rather that allow her to help him become wealthy. But like she said, he wasn't strong enough to keep a powerful woman like her.

I also recognized right then that she was too old for me to marry and build a life with. So now I was longing to find a young woman who could fulfill that role.

Sheila was the one young woman in my life who had the spiritual background and strength of character most like Carol. But I hadn't talked to Sheila since I got out of prison because I was still angry that she stopped visiting me.

I waited outside Sheila's apartment for her to leave for work. As she was about to open her car door I said "Hi Sheila" kind of quietly so I wouldn't scare her. She looked at me like she was shocked but happy to see me.

She ran up and hugged my neck and said "Hi baby, when did you get out?" I said "I've been out a while but was not sure if you wanted to see me because of the way I acted the last time you saw me." "I've been feeling bad about leaving you in there alone but I couldn't take it anymore Lashaun. I hope you forgive me" she said.

I said "Of course I forgive you but there is nothing to forgive you for. It was selfish of me to ask you to keep putting up with all the nonsense they were putting you through just to get to me.

Besides, mama never visited me. She told me the reason she did that is because I had chosen to be in prison rather than be with her. She said that she didn't believe that she left me alone but that I had left her alone. By me getting locked up in prison, in her mind, was like me choosing to be with inmates instead of her.

So I actually feel like I left you and Raven alone. I chose to do the robbery that landed me in prison. I had no right to demand that you come in there and put up with all that prison shit just because I was confined there."

Sheila hugged me again and said "Oh, you sound so sweet. Look, I am running late for work so come by later on tonight. I'm sure Raven would like to see her daddy. She is getting so big."

As I was trying to say "OK" she stepped up and kissed me. Then she jumped in the car, waved good-bye, and drove away.

I couldn't wait to see Sheila that night. I found Raven a nice big Teddy Bear and took a long hot bath before going to see her.

After eating dinner and playing with Raven a couple of hours Sheila gave her a bath and put her to bed. Then we went to bed. It felt so good being with her again but something was missing.

The love making that I was getting from Carol made being with Sheila seem common or like it was nothing special. For some reason I couldn't stop thinking about Carol and feeling like I was cheating on her by being with Sheila.

While we were laying there Sheila began asking me what had I been doing since I got back home. I told her that I had returned to the restaurant that I had been working at before.

Then without realizing what I was doing I began talking about Carol and all she had done for me. Sheila caught me off guard when she said "It sounds to me like you are sleeping with her." I said "What... what do you mean?"

She got up, started putting on her clothes, and said "You know what I mean. I see that goofy ass look on your face like you might be in love with her." I said "I like her but I'm not in love with her."

"So you did sleep with her?" Sheila asked. "Well, yeah, but…" "I knew it. You been flying around eating shit but then you bring your ass over here to land on me just like a nasty fly" she said.

She grabbed my coat and threw it at me. "When you leave, don't come back." It hurt me to leave her but I knew the love was gone so I had no choice but to leave.

A few weeks after this, and being somewhat depressed over finally losing Sheila, I spotted Monster and took care of his ass.

After killing Monster something inside of me changed and brought me right back to my old way of thinking and behaving. I kept having more thoughts of prison life, Jasmine, Mad Dog, Smiley and all of my Latin King brothers. Something inside of me was drawing me back to criminal activity.

I had a talk with Carol about how I was feeling and she asked me a question that was confusing at first. She asked me "Have you been incarcerated ever since you been out or have you been free."

I asked "What are you talking about?" She then asked the same question but in a different way "Are you still a prisoner or a free man?" I said "A free man!" She asked "Then why is your mind still in prison? Free men don't have their mind on prison."

She said "When the slave master first caught a slave he had to keep chains on him or he would run away. Once the slave accepted the fact that he was a

198

slave, the slave master could take the chains off of him because he no longer had a desire to leave.

Even when Harriet Tubman helped them get on the train to freedom some slaves would try to jump off the track and go back. She had to threaten them at gun point to keep them from going back and some she even had to kill because she knew they would tell.

The point is a free man does not become a slave until he accepts the condition of slavery in his mind. A man does not become a prisoner until he accepts the prison condition in his mind. A man does not become incarcerated once they put his body behind bars. He does not become an incarcerated until his mind becomes institutionalized.

Once a man becomes institutionalized the warden can set him free or let him go out on parole but because he is institutionalized in his mind he will always go back. You have to decide whether or not you are a prisoner. You have to recognize whether or not your mind has been institutionalized."

That made more sense to me than anything thing else she ever said to me but I still couldn't shake the thoughts. I decided to just work hard every day to distract my mind from those thoughts.

On my 22nd birthday just after my probation had ended Carol baked me a cake. I was so happy because this was my first birthday cake ever in life. Mama never baked me a birthday cake that I could remember.

Rather than eating the cake right then I wanted to eat some of that pussy. Having sex with Carol made me feel so good; like a real man.

Just being in bed lying on top of her with her under me thrusting her hips toward me making me dig down deeper into that pussy gave me a feeling of power. Her pussy actually made me feel free. We came together beautifully that night and slept peacefully for an hour or two.

Carol got up and went into the kitchen. While in there she lit the candles on the cake and came in the bedroom and grabbed me out of the bed. We were standing in the kitchen butt naked over a birthday cake.

She stood behind me and started stroking my dick and seductively said "Make a wish". She made me a little uncomfortable because as she was stroking my dick she was kind of humping on my ass at the same time.

As she was still stroking my dick with her left hand she reached between my legs with her right hand and began caressing my balls. My god that felt so good that I had to bend over slightly to rest my hands on the table. Then she slid her right hand back towards my ass and stuck her thumb right up in my asshole.

Before I knew it I punched her hard enough with my left hand to knock her to the floor. My right hand was hurting from breaking it on Monster's face so I didn't hit her as hard as I normally would have.

But I took the cake and slammed it down on her head while the candles were still lit. Then I screamed at her "Don't you ever do no shit like that again! What makes you think I want some shit stuck in my ass? You think I'm some kind of punk, bitch?"

She screamed back "Get out of my house! Get the fuck out!" I said "I'll be glad to get out of your fuckin house with you pulling some faggot shit on me." I put on my clothes quick and dashed out the door. When I left Carol was still laying on the kitchen floor crying.

I was out of a job now and had no money coming in. So I went right back to doing robberies and got enough money to start slinging product again. This time with the knowledge Carol had given me about money and business I was determined to do it in a way that would make me wealthy.

But I knew that I would need a good woman so I went on the hunt for a good one. Breaking my hand on Monster, at the moment I met her, was a like a godsend because it led me to find Lola.

Chapter 12
25

"I have really sinned. I am going to pause now,
and sit here on the mound
repenting in deepest shame..."
~ Dodie Smith

Today is my 25th birthday. I am still on the run but things are going well. I am relaxed and not feeling the pressure of being on the run. At the same time, though, I am really missing Naomi and Geselle. There is still another week or so to go before I'll know if it is safe to go back home.

I've spent the last week here in Atlanta, actually Brookhaven a suburb of Atlanta, having a good time and trying to lay low. There are so many night clubs around Atlanta with so many Black people everywhere that it is hard to avoid them.

It's not too bad though. There is a nice club with kind of a mix of different people, The Tongue and Groove, I like to go to.

There are a few White and Asian girls in there sometimes that I can pick up quick and roll out with. Once they know that you are at a really nice hotel they don't ask too many questions. I can dig their back out and drop them off without having to go through a whole trip.

203

The sisters like to try to get all up in your business too much whereas White and Asian girls just want to get a good taste of jungle love while keeping it damn near anonymous.

I picked up this hot White blonde that was into the brothers under cover. She went to clubs specifically to get picked up by Black men, let them beat the pussy up, then she would go back to her normal life.

She gave the most amazing head ever and would come while doing it. At one point she made me come from just sucking my balls as she was stroking my dick. You talk about a toe curling orgasm the girl had launched me into another world of feeling good.

The thing that was a little freaky about her is she did not like the missionary position. She said that she never had an orgasm in that position so it was a waste of time for her.

She took my index finger, stuck it in her pussy so that it was against the back wall of her clit. She said "That is my G-spot. The only way a man can really hit that good enough to make me go crazy is to turn it upside down. So doggie style is the only way I like to get down baby." She told me.

She had me find things like telephone books and shit that we could use to prop up the end of the bed so that it would come up to her waist. Then she laid her torso over the bed with her feet still on the floor and she wanted me to hit her from the back like that.

The bed and her booty were just the right height for me to dig up in that ass like I was drillin for oil. She liked to be hit hard and I didn't have enough grip with my bare feet. So I put on my Timberland's and there I was butt naked in boots killin that pussy and she was comin like crazy.

The next morning was a Sunday. After returning from dropping her back off at the club I turned on the TV and there was an advertisement that caught my attention.

It was for a Christian men's conference at the Word of Faith Family Ministries Church headed by Bishop L. Daniel West. The ad said that there would be a number of speakers and the little samples of their speeches seemed interesting.

The commercial said it was going to be held next Saturday and I thought that I should go. If it was anything thing like what I experienced at the OnCenter in Syracuse, I wanted to be there.

The first speaker who came to the stage was a Pastor who said that he used to be a Detroit gang member and drug dealer. He caught my interest immediately when he said "Men who are earning money illegally have to find a way to do it legally." He told a story that struck me and made it feel like he was speaking directly to me.

He said "There was a gangster named Lucky Luciano who was the Godfather of organized crime and the first Don of the notorious Genovese Family.

He is credited with creating the national crime syndicate (la cosa nostra; our thing) that divided criminal business activity among the 5 mafia families in New York City.

He quoted Luciano as having said "If I had it to do all over again, I would go legit. The reason why is because the intellect you need to make a million dollars illegally is the same intellect you need to make a million legally."

Then he said "You brothers out here selling drugs in the community have to understand that crime is business. You are not doing anything differently (in terms of conducting business) than what the man who owns McDonald's is doing.

Both of you are managing money, managing people, and moving a product. The big difference between you and him though is he is doing it legally but you are doing it illegally.

The money the man who owns McDonald's earns is clean. So he can afford to have a beautiful wife, a nice life, take vacations, buy a big house, and raise good kids without worrying about the police kicking his door in.

He doesn't have to be concerned with government agents and agencies taking away his possessions and destroying his family.

You have the same intellect that he does but you are making your money illegally. So you have to learn how to utilize your GOD given gifts, talents and abilities to make your money legally. This way you can earn money in a way that makes you an asset to your community rather than an enemy."

I almost wanted to cry because here I am on the run right now and can't be with my lady and baby because I'm earning my money illegally. Like he said, I have to worry about the police or government agencies breaking in my door every day just as they had before.

I'm running like a scared rabbit because I haven't found a way to change my money making operation from being an enemy in the community to an enterprise. I've got to do better than this and I can because I have the skills. I just didn't see it until now.

Mama's ex-husband Leroy provided me with a good example of how to be enterprising and I'm just now realizing it. He was a good business man in reality who would have been more successful financially if he had picked the right woman to back him.

Mama was a taker and user who didn't have the spiritual power within her, like Carol talked about, to help make a man wealthy. At least there was none that I could see.

I think that I got lucky finding Geselle. I can tell she has that power in her but it will be up to me to bring it out of her. Right now I got her fucked up doing shit illegally.

Together we have the capacity to make a million dollars legally. I have to make sure that we find a way to get out of crime and go legit for our baby.

As I was sitting there thinking about how to do business legally another speaker had come to the stage. He broke me out of my imagination and self pity back to reality when I heard him say that he was going to speak for a few minutes on channeling your sexual energy.

He said "The average Black man fails in life, love and business because we have not learned to channel our sexual energy.

Most of us, he said, are being crippled financially because we have to pay money to support a child that is outside of our family. That divided money is creating division in our marriages for those of us who are married and is depriving us of the power to become wealthy.

It is said that all money ain't good money but I'm here to tell you that all pussy ain't good pussy!" The men in the crowd erupted in laughter, cheers and were doing that Arsenio Hall dog pound call.

I don't know what is happening but it seems like this whole conference was put together just for me. Here is another man that seems to be calling me out or speaking to me directly.

He said "A man's power is centered between his waist and mid thigh. The reason most men are not MORE successful is because they have not learned to

208

harness their power or channel their sexual energy. They divide the majority of their waking hours between chasing cash and coochie.

The energy one needs to get cash is the same energy they use to get coochie. If they can learn to properly channel their sexual energy into chasing cash rather than getting coochie they would have a lot more cash."

I'm seeing what he is saying to be so true because when I was chasing cash and coochie I was always broke. But when I was keeping regular hours hustling and coming home in the evening to Lola or Geselle, I started making a lot more money.

In fact, with both of them (Geselle more than Lola though) I had more money than I could actually spend. Dam this cat is on point.

He said "Now, a woman is a man's key to becoming wealthy. The Bible says who can FIND a virtuous woman, her price (or value) is far above rubies.

The definition of the word "virtue" in this context is: strength, power and moral excellence. Placing value (not a price) on the vagina positions you to move into and take advantage of a woman's virtue.

Men place a higher value on a woman who has placed a high value on her vagina. Because she is conservative with it she demonstrates that she has strength, power and moral excellence and proves by doing so that she is worth that value.

A man with a true business mind knows that he can take his business to a much greater level of earning when he has a woman of virtue. The problem most business minded men have is, though, it is very hard to find a woman of virtue.

It's easy for business men to get pussy because they have money, power and other things. If pussy was a commodity on the stock market however its value would be dropping everyday because too many women just GIVE it away and their virtue along with it.

Getting a woman of virtue is not that easy. A woman's virtue (or strength, power, moral excellence) is directly connected to her vagina.

Controlling the activity in there preserves her virtue and increases her value. She can use pussy to get money but wealth is linked to the value of her vagina and how she uses the power associated with it.

If a woman wants to start having a higher class of men, men with real power and money, she has to learn to have confidence and radiate grace and inner beauty which are signs of virtue. And she has to stop being so quick to give up the booty."

He went on to say that "There is a difference between adult sized boys and a man. Real men place a high value on a woman of virtue.

There is also a difference between adult sized females and a woman. Adult sized females have a pussy but a real woman owns a vagina; one has a toy

210

that she uses to get money and boys and the other has a tool that she uses to obtain power.

Kim Kardashian has pussy but Michelle Obama has power! The ladies who learn to understand the power in virtue will be able to attract and marry a powerful man like Michelle too."

The men in the crowd are going wild now, laughing, yelling, and smacking each other up. I was enjoying it too but it was hitting me so hard that I couldn't help but take what he was saying seriously.

I started thinking to myself, this is some high tech pimp shit! These cats are amazing. Things Carol taught me about money were good but hers was first grade compared to these guys.

I wish I would have heard this or had a man tell me this kind of stuff earlier. Maybe I would have made some better choices.

I am in the habit of slinging my dick all over the place just trying to get some pussy. I can see now that some of that wasted energy may have landed me in prison.

If I hadn't had a baby early maybe I wouldn't have needed to steal so much money. If I wasn't so focused on looking cool for the honies, I probably wouldn't have done a robbery to get money to rent a stolen car. Maybe I never would have gotten caught in it and maybe I never would have gone to prison. It seems like it has always been the pursuit of pussy and money that has been driving me.

The man is right. All money ain't good money and all pussy ain't good pussy. A good pussy is one that is good for you not one that feels good to you.

This shit is real talk for the right time. I have to do something to use this to not only change my mind, the way I have been thinking, but also to change my money or the way I've been earning it. This is some heavy shit!

I couldn't stay in my seat anymore. Something inside of me was moving so I had to get up and walk around.

There was so much on my mind now and it seemed like I was going into information overload from taking everything in and thinking about what I am going to do. That is, until the next speaker, who had a Jamaican or African accent, caught my attention.

"My brothers, he said, we are struggling in this thing we call Christianity. As a result murder, crime, and poverty are running rampant in our community. I believe this is due largely to preachers giving people a false sense of security.

They teach that GOD forgives all sin like there is not a price to pay attached to it. This sounds good but the truth is sin always has a price attached to it.

GOD will forgive your sins once you TRULY repent but the devil is always going to make sure that you pay. Once you are in the devil's gang and have been committing sin, you can't just leave. You've gotta get JUMPED out!"

I immediately thought of Smiley and the Latin Kings. "Oh, shit!" I said to myself. "This is straight up gangsta shit!"

He said "The wages of sin is DEATH. In the court room of heaven when we sin the devil, the accuser (or prosecutor) of the brethren, always argues for the highest penalty allowable by law: DEATH!

The word says he accuses or files charges against us but it doesn't say they are false charges. The charges he files are true. But Jesus, (the public defender) the Wonderful Counselor, argues for an alternative sentence.

But, because the wages of sin is death something has to die. Sometimes that death, thanks be to Jesus, shows up as our car dying, there may be the death of peace in our home, a member of our family, a relationship, our financial well being, but something has to die. This is why the baby that David and Bathsheba birthed in sin had to die."

Now I'm starting to get scared. I love my baby Naomi so much and I don't want anything I've done to cause her to die.

Next he said "Job is a classic example. He was described as an upright man; one who avoided evil. However, he unknowingly got involved in practicing a form of witchcraft.

Most preachers don't know how to read the word well enough to understand this is what happened even though it is there plain as day.

Job ended up losing ALL his possessions and ALL of his children. Now, once he truly repented GOD gave him double for his trouble.

That was because Job had a good heart, had always intended to do good, and didn't realize he was doing evil. BUT he HAD to pay the penalty even though he didn't really realize what he was doing."

Before I knew it tears started rolling down my eyes because I was still thinking about my baby girl. A man next to me saw my tears, wiped his eyes and said "I know, man, I'm feelin it too." I said "I'm not crying, my eyes are just sweating." He said "Yeah, mine too." We bumped shoulders together, dapped each other up, and laughed.

The man on stage was still going on with his hard hitting speech saying "People who go to church EVERY week are continually engaging in sin and their lives are jacked-up because their preachers tell them that GOD is going to forgive them.

Because the penalty for their sin often falls a long time after the sin was committed they think that GOD has forgiven them. The court room of heaven has a heavy case backlog just like the courts in the earth. So once the penalty for sin comes upon them they can't understand what they are experiencing or why when the judgment hits their lives.

They don't understand what is happening because their preachers haven't helped them properly understand the word. It is amazing to me how people swear THEIR preacher is so anointed and THEIR preacher knows the word so well.

Yet, crime, poverty, and murder have a strong foothold in the community surrounding his church's door! People have to wake up and realize that if THEIR preacher knew the word better (just him or her alone), the entire Black community would be doing better.

The problem church going people have is they are doing more PREACHER worship than GOD worship. They don't understand that THEIR preacher DON'T know the word that well so they lead the people to depend too heavily on emotion and wishful thinking rather than the truth of the word.

GOD will forgive you, my brothers, but the devil is ALWAYS going to argue to get his due. What most preachers don't know and we don't realize is GOD is even being merciful with us when HE allows the devil to get his due. That means that that debt for sin is then paid in full and we won't have to pay that penalty again on Judgment Day."

I lost track of what he was saying for a while because I started looking back over my life and thinking about how all of this applied directly to me.

Maybe my going to prison was the devil getting his due. Prison was the death of my freedom that came due for all the robberies.

I was thinking to myself how much more debt for sin have I left to pay. I have done a lot. I've hurt and killed a lot of people. How will I ever pay off this debt without it affecting Geselle and Naomi?

Then I heard him say "Think about this as you prepare for Bible Study this week: Most people believe that getting saved is all they have to do in order to please GOD or get into heaven. But, salvation is only the FIRST step to pleasing or to being in righteousness with GOD.

After you are saved you MUST go through a process of conversion (Matthew 18:3 & Luke 22:32) from being in the world to being in Christ (Romans 12:1-2). Then, you MUST go through a process of: restoration, installation, operation and glorification (Romans 8:30 & 2 Thessalonians 1:12).

That means to be restored to the person GOD intended you to be, to stand in the place GOD intended you to occupy, doing what GOD intended you to do, and completing the purpose you were sent here to fulfill.

That is how we achieve glorification while we yet live or IN the earth as it is in Heaven. It is vital that we each reach glorification or FINISH the work we were sent here to do or we will never hear "Well done, thy good and faithful servant, enter ye into the joy of the Lord."

Once we glorify GOD, HE will glorify us IN earth or in this earthen vessel while we are still ON earth. But HE will also glorify us in Heaven.

This is how we "obtain" the right as sons and daughters of GOD to have the power, protection, provision, prosperity and peace of GOD in Heaven while we are on earth."

I'm starting to really cry now because I know that I need this power, protection, provision, prosperity and peace. But I don't know how to get it.

I make my money through crime and don't know how to convert that crime into a legal enterprise. I want to stop committing sin right now but I still have 10 kilos of cocaine that I have to move. That is close to a million dollars that I cannot just throw away. At the same time, that much cocaine going into folk's brains will hurt a lot of people.

I want to be through with hurting people. I am so confused right now that I don't know what to do.

At this point the Bishop came to the stage and offered men to come to Jesus Christ by asking for salvation and forgiveness. I threw my hands up and gave my life to Christ right there. I couldn't help it because I felt like I had to; I needed to.

Then, the Bishop began asking for an offering. He said "I want any man who has a thousand dollars or more to give to come down front." I had 30 $100 dollar bills in my pocket and decided to put it all into the collection.

As I reached the front with some other men the Bishop said "Stand next to Deacon Rogers and he is going to pray for you." When I pulled the wad of $100s out of my pocket the Deacon asked "How much is this?" I said "About $3,000 dollars."

He excitedly announced to the Bishop "We have an offering of $3,000!" The Bishop said "Praise the Lord!" and the crowd kind of murmured.

I was starting to feel sort of embarrassed because I didn't want this kind of attention. The Deacon asked me "What do you want me to pray for?" I said "I don't know. I am so confused."

He said "I tell you what. I will have you talk to the Bishop and he will help you figure it out." I thought to myself "Yes, it might help to have a man of GOD who put on a conference that affected me so powerfully give me some advice to help me figure out what to do or where to go from here."

I was feeling so convicted that I knew I had to do something. I was starting to feel better now.

I waited about 40 minutes and everybody was just about gone before the Deacon led me back into the Bishop's office. The Deacon introduced me to the Bishop. He shook my hand, hugged me, and asked "What can I do for you?"

At that moment I became overwhelmed with grief. I just kneeled down, starting crying, and said "I don't know what to do!" I began to ask him to ask GOD to forgive my life and all the things I had done. The Bishop nodded to the Deacon who smiled and then left the office.

The Bishop started telling me about love, GOD's forgiveness, and that it was GOD's plan for man to receive love from other men in these situations.

He said "It is our duty to restore one another to GOD though love and only men can do that for other men." I started feeling uncomfortable now because this cat was acting kind of funny.

My suspicion was confirmed when he started rubbing my head seductively. I wanted to receive repentance and a new me but this nigga made the old me rise back up quickly.

I stood up and grabbed his hand making him think I wanted to hold it. Then I used it to quickly bend back his wrist which causes great pain.

This is a technique the CO's used in prison called a pain compliance hold when they wanted to take down a prisoner who was out of control.

I took him down quick and he landed on his back. I kept control over his arm by locking his elbow across my knee in a bar. I put my foot on his neck and stepped down hard until he choked out.

I picked him up, put him on the couch, and covered him with a blanket that was in there to make it appear he was just sleeping. Then, I quickly snuck out of the place being careful not to be seen and left.

As I was driving back to the hotel, I was so mad I didn't know what to do. "This punk muthafucka thought I was a faggot. Why the fuck did he think that I was gay?" I yelled to myself.

"He is lucky that choking his bitch ass is all I had time to do to him. Now, I have to get out of town and go on the run again."

I shot back to the hotel, packed in a hurry, and checked out. By the time I hit I-75 going towards Marietta I was still fuming.

"All that church shit them niggas was feeding me with and this muthafuckin Bishop turns out to be a punk faggot ass molester.

Well, no more molesting young men or boys for you muthafucka... nasty bitch! I hope you prayed for forgiveness while I was choking your bitch ass out!"

Just then I heard one of the burners in my bag ping that I had a text. It was from Geselle and it said "Clean".

"YEEEESSSS, I yelled. Right on, muthafuckin, time!" I'm on my way back home to be with my lady and my baby.

Domestic violence is a serious crime that could lead to death. It affects all kinds of people regardless of gender, ethnicity, race, sexual orientation or religion.

Domestic abusers use intimidation and fear to gain power and control over their victims and may use children, pets, threats, and isolation to maintain power and control.

1 in 4 women and 1 in 14 men are seriously hurt or killed by their spouse or partner in the U.S. every year.

If your partner is controlling or physically, mentally or emotionally abusive, don't ignore or try to excuse their behavior. Please seek help immediately.

Call 911 if you're in immediate danger and teach your children how to call 911 in an emergency.

Call the National Domestic Hotline for information on how you can receive help in your local area:
(800)799-7233
or
(800)787-3224 TTY for the hearing/speech impaired.

www.ingramcontent.com/pod-product-compliance
Lightning Source LLC
Chambersburg PA
CBHW070623130626
46556CB00001B/452